everything I WANTED

evey lyon

EVERHOPE ROAD

Everything I Wanted

Everything I Dreamed

Everything I Needed

Copyright © 2024 by Evey Lyon

Written and published by: Evey Lyon, Lost Compass Press

Edited by: Contagious Edits

Proofreading: Rachel Rumble

Cover Design: Lily Bear Design Co.

All rights reserved.

No part of this book may be reproduced in any form or by any electronic or mechanical means. Including information storage and retrieval systems, without written permission from the author, except for the use of brief quotations in a book review.

This book is a work of fiction. The names, characters, places, and incidents are products of the writer's imagination and used fictitiously and are not to be perceived as real. Any resemblance to persons, venues, events, businesses are entirely coincidental.

The author acknowledges the trademark status and trademark owners of various products referenced in this work of fiction, which have been used without permission. The publication/use of these trademarks is not authorized, associated with, or sponsored by the trademark owner.

The author expressly prohibits using this work in any manner for purposes of training artificial intelligence technologies to generate text, including without limitation, technologies that are capable of generating works in the same style or genre as this work. The author reserves all rights to license uses of this work for generative AI training and development of machine learning language models.

Author's Note: No artificial intelligence (A.I.) or predictive language software was used in any part of the creation of this book.

This book is U.S. copy registered and further protected under international copyright laws.

ABOUT

It started with my grumpy neighbor being enemy number one. The cocky uptight lawyer always seems to swagger my way with a disgruntled look and piercing eyes when my mail continues to get accidentally delivered to his house. Keats always makes me feisty and annoyed, too. Hence why we're both always in a showdown where I want to rip his shirt into shreds and maybe his pants, too. Why? Because the attraction is too overbearing and lingers in the air.

And then we snap and give in.

We start the unimaginable. We unintentionally start a neighbors-with-benefits kind of thing. But I begin to see a different side of Keats, and it turns out he isn't the kind of man I thought he was. The fact that he turns possessive or moves me right in due to a house complication tells me that he feels something, too. We're blindsided by our relationship developing, and neither one of us is sure where this will end. After all, we never planned on being everything I wanted...

KEATS

I'm tempted.
By the situation.
The package, I mean.

I want to take the knife in my hand and destroy yet another box that arrived at my house because either the delivery man hasn't learned from his mistakes yet or there is simply someone incapable of doing their job writing the correct address on a package. This should have arrived to my pain-in-the-ass neighbor. This must be the third box in a week.

Every. Single. Time. I must come face to face with my nemesis.

For unexplainable reasons, it was hate at first sight with the woman who has a permanent scowl when she crosses my path. The woman who has a perfect curve to her shoulder with smooth skin, because Esme wants to be a little temptress and wear off-the-shoulder t-shirts. Sometimes her dirty blonde hair is down or other times up in a messy bun that would still be suitable for my hand to yank her head back to shut her up with my tongue down her throat. Even better, my cock.

Alas, her not-so-stellar personality prevents me from crossing any lines.

Fine.

Today, I will not stab a sharp object into this box with a return address from someplace in Washington state. A far place from here in Everhope, Illinois. I live far enough from Chicago and close enough to my sister and my work for the hockey team, the Spinners, in Lake Spark.

I deal enough with arrogant and cocky people in the hockey industry. Luckily, my cutthroat approach to all legal matters as the team's legal counsel keeps me from throwing a chair at anyone.

Everhope doesn't have a lake; we have a serene river surrounded by green trees to escape for a little calm.

The calm only lasts so long. Because every time I turn onto Everhope Road—since whoever named these streets had zero creativity—I lose my peace, and I haven't even lived here for a year.

My phone vibrating on the counter causes me to abandon the knife.

I see it's my buddy, Oliver. He also works with me, which begs the question, "Business or personal?" I ask because we work together on the legal team.

"Geez, what a welcome greeting, Keats." I can hear the humor in his voice.

My brows rise as I shake off my thoughts. "Sorry." I take one deep breath. "How are you doing today? The birds singing? Coffee still good at Foxy Rox?" My feigned chipper tone causes him to laugh.

"Damn, what's gotten into you? And fine, yes, and yes."

"Okay. It's Saturday, what is up?"

"Well, I'm calling on a personal note."

My forehead creases. "Not working hard enough?" Normally, Saturdays turn into a workday.

"Nah, I'll look at the contracts later. Just wanted to check if you want to head to the gym or go for a run? May weather is treating us well."

Drawing a line from the unopened box out the living room window, I notice the dreaded car of doom approaching. "Not today. I need to be graced with Esme's presence due to yet another mail mishap."

Oliver chuckles under his breath. "If I hear about a murder on the news then I am not your alibi. But after your argument that the neighbors will watch for entertainment, we can still meet up. Maybe throw some burgers on the grill." Oliver lives down the street which means it's a quick walk.

Dragging my eyes away from the window, I begin to saunter toward the door, tucking the box under my arm. "I really can't. I need to shop online and find a few gifts my nephew." That soft spot in my heart that does exist, warms with fondness. My little sister Summer and I are close. She's been through a lot, and I'm brother bear. Even if that means accepting the new man in her life, Nash, the brother of her late husband who passed last year. But my nephew, Bo? That little one-year-old guy steals the show.

"Fine. But I'll probably call later for business," Oliver says.

"Later." I end the call and set my cell on the side table by the front door.

Deep breath. It's about to begin.

Swinging the door open, I begin to charge my way to my not-so-lovely next-door neighbor's driveway. Esme is halfway to standing with her car door open when she notices me, and the eye roll must be instinctual.

"What now?" Dread floods her voice. She pushes her door shut with disgruntled energy. I'm more gentle with my car, but to each to their own.

Holding up the box, my unimpressed facial expression should already explain it all to her. "When the fuck will this stop, Miss Pines?" *And when will you stop wearing jeans that mold to your body, with your hair framing your face with those whispering gray eyes?*

Her hands find her hips. "Well, when will you be a normal welcoming neighbor, Mr. Roth?" She moved in a few months ago, taking the house from her aunt Margerie who left her the place in her will.

My eyes bug out. "Says the woman who gave everyone on the street a cherry pie except me."

She snickers. "You don't deserve one. Besides, I forgot that you live here. Just assumed it's your holiday house. Don't you normally reside by the gates of Hell?"

I pinch the bridge of my nose with my free hand. "Oh, because you are such an angel, making the dirtiest choice of desserts. Pie. Really?" I scoff. "Following the cliché pin-up girl vibe?"

She points her finger at me with a glare to accompany it. "Who the fuck brings a sexual reference to baking a pie? Oh… oh yeah, the neighbor who can take his fine suits and his noisy car to another street. Shall I arrange the for-sale sign for your yard?"

I stand taller to correct her. "It's a Ferrari, so yeah, I'm going to rev the engine."

"Is that what you say to women when you are about to deliver your 30 second performance?" she asks dryly.

We both step closer, the tension boiling as it always does in one another's presence.

"Actually, the clock doesn't have enough numbers to time me. Would you like references?"

"Ugh, you are piece of work," she grumbles.

In the corner of my eye, I notice old lady Mrs. Tiller staring at us from next door to Esme's house, pretending to garden. And Kelly from across the street? I just learned to ignore that she's always watching us and standing by her garage still holding the leash to her Labrador. The dog just sits there with his ears perked, staring at us. Oh hell, did her husband just come out to enjoy his cup of coffee and watch the scene?

Doesn't matter. I shove the box to Esme, and she snatches it out of my arms.

"Fix this mail situation," I grind out.

Her eyes grow big. "Not my fault the mail system could use improvements. I bet you don't even give the mailman holiday cards."

Shaking my head, I'm now in agony. We can only go in circles for so long.

"What is even in these envelopes and boxes?"

Esme's head lolls to the side. "Things for work. Some of us actually have a happy job. Bringing joy to others instead of spitting out boring legal terms, or even worse, defending douchebag hockey players who get caught cheating, with photos online to prove it."

I step even closer at that reminder. We still haven't found the culprit of leaking the photo, nor do we care, as you can't destroy facts. Still, it was a PR nightmare, and to be honest, dealing with the player's shitty behavior was not my happiest day, but in truth, it was a career win on many fronts considering I got to bill extra hours. "Really? Low blows?"

"Fine… the packages are lenses for my camera or hardware for my laptop. Photographers need these things. Other times, the boxes are just heavy blunt objects in case I need to murder you. I'm stocking up." Pure attitude is written all over her face.

I sigh, exhausted. "Well, you can save your money on the handcuffs. You can borrow mine." As soon as that flies out of my mouth, she inhales a sharp breath. We pause and both seem to ponder something, and we probably shouldn't share what.

Her tongue swipes along her teeth, and she pretends to look down at the address on the box. "Aren't you the gentleman," she says softly, sarcastic.

Rubbing my face in my hands, I debate if we should end this Saturday quarrel yet. But I get my kicks out of making her day miserable.

"I'm serious. Fix this address situation." *Or don't.*

Her shoulders rise. "I have. Well… at least the address part. I double-check and recheck when I enter my details. Maybe the automatic system thing when you enter a zip code changes it on their end."

I throw her a pointed look. "Yet, everything is fine on my end. Are you receiving my mail?" My finger lands on my chin to contemplate. "No," I sharply inform her.

Esme growls again. "That's not true and you know it. I got one of your envelopes the other week. Anyhow, I would say sorry, but you're incapable of feelings and manners."

One more step. This time from her end. Bringing us dangerously too close, my cologne and her light flowery perfume mixing.

"Hmm. Funny that." I glance to my side. "Kelly, didn't I bring the best of the best Blisswood wine to your holiday party and treats for your dog, all while giving you a genuine smile?" I call out.

"Uh... yeah?" she answers, hesitant to enter the conversation.

I whip my eyes back to Esme. "See? I did that because I have manners."

Esme tucks the small box under her arms and brings her hands up for a slow clap. "Bravo. One little thing."

"All good? Assuming this is our regular Saturday showdown on the lawn." We both turn our heads to look at Sheriff Carter jogging in place. He's Oliver's brother and moved a while back from Lake Spark a few towns over.

"Arrest him for being a menace to society." Esme gives him a pointed look.

"No can do, Esme. I'm off-duty and value my work-life balance." He flashes her a smile full of teeth.

Esme growls like a child as Carter continues his run.

"So, when people enter your house, do you just cast a spell on them to treat you like the greatest gift on earth?" I've heard the rumors of her offering tea and chats, not to mention people are always going in and out of her house. I'm not even sure what's in there except a kitchen where she bakes pies that I've never tasted.

She purses her lips, not pleased. "I have a studio for photoshoots, you despicable creature. I believe I've explained that before."

"Maybe. I didn't take an interest."

Esme's head tilts just enough to dare me. Lucky for her, we have an audience, so I can't eye-fuck her to my normal standards.

"Do you know what kind of photography I do?"

"Don't particularly care."

Her lips curl into a smirk that is borderline sultry. "Engagement photos when outside, but inside..." She clicks her tongue. "Boudoir photos. Classy yet effective gifts for women's significant others or for themselves to build confidence. Do you know what boudoir photos are?"

Internally, I groan and attempt to keep it together as the term rings a bell... or I just abused the search engine bar on my laptop once and came to the conclusion that it's classy porn. I don't answer, and that just seems to thrill her more.

"It's when you either wear lingerie or next to nothing. Heels optional."

My entire body tightens, holding on for dear life. She's taunting me, and that seems to delight her. Such a demon.

Unaffected. Act unaffected and send that message to my dick stat.

"Classy," I retort.

One moment. Two moments. We both say nothing, but our eyes lock.

"Next time I throw the package away," I whisper.

"Then you really are the neighbor from Hell."

We both step back, and she begins to walk briskly away.

"Have a lovely day," I mention with a contrite smile.

My body finally relaxes, and when I turn to return to my house, I notice eyes from neighbors quickly finding the ground. Great. We'll be the talk of the next neighborhood association meeting.

The moment, I'm in my house with the door closed, I mosey my way to the kitchen to peruse the fridge.

How the fuck is this situation sustainable for my sanity?

I guess I'll bury myself in some work this afternoon. Maybe call an old fuck buddy to work out my frustration, but for some indescribable reason, that doesn't seem appealing. My neighbor is indeed the worst human on earth since she ruined my ability to fuck someone senseless.

I do not appreciate her getting under my skin. I'm a lawyer, after all.

It's 11:56 on the oven clock. Fuck it. I pull out a bottle of Matchbox IPA, a brew from Sage Creek, from the middle shelf then close the fridge. Popping the cap off with the nearby opener, I take a deep swallow; the taste of alcohol is soothing.

A few minutes later, I'm sitting on the edge of the couch, stationed behind my laptop on the coffee table and am not surprised with my full email inbox or the fact that Scotty Smith is getting traded due to the PR nightmare. I don't condone cheating, so I have no problem whipping through the needed legal papers to get him on a plane out of here for a player trade.

This is how my weekends go. Gym, beer, work, and to make it riveting, add in arguments with my neighbor for my breaks from my laptop.

Sitting up and straightening my spine, I comb my fingers through my hair. For some peculiar reason my lips quirk out, and I tap my finger loudly on the table.

And fuck my mind for betraying me and for a millisecond imagining my neighbor splayed out on it.

Because I absolutely, completely, utterly can't stand that woman.

2

ESME

"He still has no clue that you know who took the photo?" Hailey smirks as she twirls a teabag in her mug.

I only recall for a brief second how I discovered this tidbit from another photographer in the area. She's someone I'm acquainted with from a local meet-up group of photographers.

Hailey's been my friend forever. I've known her since we were teenagers. Her school year is winding down for her middle schoolers, and she'll only teach a few days a week for summer school. She can relax more, which means sitting on my couch with our feet under our knees and leaning into the sofa is a regular occurrence. Sometimes wine shows up too.

"Nah. I'm saving it for the perfect time to really piss Keats off. The fact that I encouraged her to leak the photo that probably sent the Spinners legal department into a frenzy is a card I plan on keeping in my back pocket." I glance down to my tea that I don't really want. I would much prefer a coffee from Foxy Rox. Cold-pressed coffee all the way.

Hailey narrows her eyes at me. "You two are playing some twisted game."

Sighing, I reach to the side table to set my mug down. "It's not a game. It's a nightmare. I think the zip code auto-fills addresses on their end. You know how we added the dash plus numbers to our five-digit codes a few years back? It messed with all the automations. Sometimes I get Mrs. Tiller's boxes, too."

"Probably."

Tugging my hairband off, I let my hair loose. "I just wish I didn't have to cross his path so much. Such an arrogant guy. He's married to his work and seems to be wound tightly, grumpy too."

She hums a noise. "Well, at least he's easy on the eyes, your eyes in particular."

Something tightens in a place that I wish he had zero effect on. The truth hurts sometimes, but yes, okay, he's lean yet toned, and his crisp white shirts with two buttons loose at the top brings out his whiskey-brown eyes. I choose not to comment on the way his chocolatey-brown hair, short in the back but just long enough on top, would probably be nice to sink my fingers into.

Shaking the image out of my head, I raise my brows at my friend. "I guess he's alright, if that's your type."

Hailey stares at me blankly.

Divert. Divert. Divert.

"*So.*" I lean forward to slap her arm gently. "That party at the manor you have happening. Do tell."

Excitement floods her face. She volunteers at the historical museum outside Everhope, and she managed to steal a slot on the busy calendar to throw a birthday party for her brother. "Of course, we're going to theme with the times of the manor, so 1920s. Long table for dinner with high candles. But I think we are going to add a murder mystery to the mix."

I roll my eyes because it's ridiculous, yet I love it. "Let me guess... we need costumes?"

She claps her hands together once. "Absolutely. I'm also going to send invites by mail, too. None of that e-mail or chat message crap. We're going all in."

A smile breaks out on my lips. "This is kind of cool. Although we know how I feel about haunted places." My eyes draw up to the ceiling.

She sputters a laugh. "Still think this place is possessed?"

"Uhm, not really. I just can't help shake that there might be a curse or something. Something doomed to happen." Ghosts are not my thing, but there is an uneasy feeling that sometimes breezes into the air here. My great aunt was lovely, and thanks to her, I get a home mortgage free. It's just strange because my old great-aunt never mentioned that this two-story house with a front porch and farm-styled kitchen would ever be mine. My home is by far better than my neighbor's wraparound porch, a house way too large for one, but I guess Keats needs room to put his ego somewhere.

It's just every now and then I feel a brisk breeze that chills down my spine. Something of the past or something foreshadowing the future. Not going to lie, I've been burning sage a lot.

"I promise it will be fun. I need to figure out which characters everyone will be." Hailey seems to be reflecting, as she's in her element of party planning, but then her face turns pained. "Right, so you know that Keats is a friend of my brother which means that Keats is also getting an invite."

Rolling my eyes, I choose to take the high road. "Sure. Kind of expected that."

Relief hits her. "Great. I really want this to be a great birthday for Liam. He's going to pop the question to Ava. I helped him pick the ring." I don't really know Ava, but from what Hailey tells me, she's okay.

"That's lovely. I should bring my camera, but I kind of want to enjoy the night."

She touches my knee. "Absolutely. Besides, it might be more authentic if we all have our cells secretly recording instead. More element of surprise, you know?"

"Totally. That reminds me, I need to go over a client's mood boards. I have this cute couple who just graduated from college and got engaged, and they want photos by the riverboat downtown. Then there is a new mom who wants to shoot boudoir pictures as a present for an anniversary."

Both Hailey and I are single, which is probably why there is a short pause as we consider what life would be like with someone.

But life is okay with a happy job and hobbies, right? You shouldn't rush for more in life.

Which reminds me. "Still haven't hooked up with Oliver yet?" He's her brother's best friend and also Keats's friend and colleague, but I won't hold that against Oliver. Besides, he lives down the street, and I can use friendly neighbors.

"No." She draws it out and in the most awkward of tones. "Don't be crazy. Liam would go through the roof."

My fingers tap a pillow. "I don't think you care."

She stands abruptly but still maintains her grin. "On that note, I need to head to my parents'. My mom is going overboard with lasagna for family night again."

"Yum." Swinging my legs off the couch, I follow her as she travels to the front door. "Enjoy."

Hailey opens her arms for a hug. "Take it easy this weekend." She tips her nose over my shoulder. "Don't forget your box that caused a front lawn battle earlier."

I nod my head as I open the door. "I won't."

We say goodbye, and when I close the door, I rest back against it with a deep sigh. It's nice that she has family nearby. They invite me over all the time, but it's not the same. My parents move around due to my dad working in a high position for a manufacturer company, and our infrequent communication feels dull at times. More like, forced basic communication that we feel we are supposed to do, not particularly engrossing. When I got my great-aunt's house, I decided to keep my roots here. Not to mention, I studied at Hollows, not so far from here, so returning to Everhope felt timely.

It's just different without family.

Dragging my feet, I head to the kitchen, picking up the box on my table near the bottom of the stairs to take it along. Once I'm in the kitchen, I grab scissors to break the tape. I'm confident that half the time when deliveries arrive looking as though they've been through a tornado, Keats is actually the one responsible. It seems today he let it be. Nothing exciting awaits me when I find the contents. Only a new mouse for my computer for when I edit photos.

I push it all to the side and scan the kitchen, debating if now is the time to get to work or do something else. Opting for work, I spend two hours looking at mood boards. A dilemma always presents itself when it comes to the boudoir shoots. Lingerie sites are part of the process. Most of the time they order from Piper's boutique over in Lake Spark. Such beautiful things. I consider myself striking in looks, and I'm by no means shy, either. Wearing lingerie in front of a camera is quite liberating, except I'm on the other side of the lens.

Clicking away the sight of fluorescent yet classy green lace bras, I hate myself for turning toward the window and letting my eyes linger for a beat.

Growling to myself for that action, I return to the kitchen

and stomp to the island and lean over to grab my blender from the low cupboard.

Baking a pie. Yes, that's what I will do to work out some frustration from today.

Setting music on my speakers and pulling out all of the ingredients, I double-check that I have canned cherries. Normally I use berries, but I don't have any fresh ones on hand, and I have zero desire to get in the car to drive to the store. Every knead of pie crust works out aggression, every stir of sugar and fruit nearly slides the bowl off the counter due to my blunt movements, and pouring cherries into the dish could be done more elegantly.

While the pie bakes, I clean the house a little and fold clothes. Boring mundane weekend tasks. It's 45 minutes later when I pull the pie out to cool. Cleaning up the house is always calming to me. I'm not a total neat freak, I just enjoy a weekly clean. I'll probably paint my nails later and watch a movie. I'm not a fan of drinking alone, though I would rather enjoy a bottle in good company.

Which most definitely is *not* with the neighbor who just started the engine to his car. What the fuck, Keats? Must I hear it from inside my home? Are you now pressing the accelerator while sitting in park to piss me off? Storming to the window in the living room, I'm too slow, and my cheeks puff out when I see his taillights as he drives away.

Why does it rile me up? Why does *he* rile me up?

Marching back to the kitchen, the empty box catches my eye, and I glance back to the living room window.

I'm so irritated right now.

My phone pings, and I walk to the other side of the counter where it's on a charger. There is a notification, and on the screen, I see the mood board app has given a suggestion of what to add.

F-you lingerie in a turquoise color.

Roaring a sound that represents an unexplainable frustration, I grab the pie cutter and yank the pie closer to me, and it only gives slight satisfaction that Keats will never get a piece.

So why the hell am I now stabbing the baked good with the utensil in my hand?

I'm in this temperament because of my neighbor. I don't act crazy when I'm normal, I swear. I'm sweet, really. I even have the tiniest bit of guilt somewhere inside me that my neighbor will never be on the receiving end of my pie.

No. Oh no. Why did that sympathetic thought come to me?

It's simple.

Keats is truly the worst person on the earth.

ESME

Must fate be so cruel?

It's been a few days since I've crossed paths with my next-door neighbor who just walked into the Foxy Rox, our local coffee spot. He most definitely deserves someone spilling coffee on him, too.

I sink into my seat at a small table by the window and raise my laptop screen a smidgen, but pretending I can hide will only buy me a minute tops. At least he didn't come in alone. He's with Oliver, and they seem to be talking business, as they are both in suits. Did Keats shave today? I can't tell.

Snap out of it. You don't care.

"Seriously, I promise you, at 2am someone will call that we need to check the contract. They are going to do a player extension and want to finalize that before another team snatches him up," Keats explains to Oliver. I have no clue who they are talking about, and I'm sure I shouldn't be eavesdropping, but this place is quiet considering it's a weekday at 8am.

"I bet you a grand that you're wrong," Oliver counters because these guys have money to blow.

Keats tips his head to the teenager behind the counter as a greeting. "Double shot of espresso." He turns to look at Oliver, but he pauses and his eyes narrow. Damn it. I've been found. "Isn't this going to be a fine day." He's not thrilled as he grinds his teeth and begins to stride my way.

Oliver glances back over his shoulder to see me, and I can hear him utter "*Shit*" under his breath. "Here goes the next twenty minutes of my life." Oliver turns to the barista. "Can you add a muffin to my order? Might as well get comfortable since I'll be watching my dear old friend have a little lovers' squabble." Right now, I want to throw something at Oliver for that comment, but I need him alive so that one day Hailey can finally live out her fantasy.

Keats and I turn to Oliver with a death stare, and he sighs then walks away. But Keats then daggers his sight to me, and I seem to be a target.

I shut my laptop with vigor and scowl at Keats. "Double shot? Really? Guess you can't manage a bullseye anyhow."

His brow rises. "Considering my ruthless approach to law with an excellent track record, then I'll assume your mind is a little filthy for 8am. So, in that case…" He arrives at my table and sets his hands on the back of the opposite chair. "It's double because why have only one round when you can have two? It leaves everyone satisfied." His innuendo burns me inside with exasperation and curiosity.

"Fine. Espresso as dark as your heart."

"I thought I didn't have a heart. I'm quite positive you've mentioned that once or twice." The barista arrives with his to-go cup, and Keats takes it without batting an eye as they remain staked at me.

I begin to stir the stick in my coffee cup to keep my hands busy. "I don't particularly care to go over the anatomy of your body, right now." I swear I hear Oliver nearly choking.

Keats only takes a moment to glance over at his friend now sitting in the corner before he returns his swaggered eyes to me, the corner of his mouth twitching with an underlying smirk. "Working on your inappropriate-for-public-spaces photos?"

"Are you attempting to have a normal conversation with me?" I say flatly as I look down at the table, pretending to be unaffected. "And they are not inappropriate. Most would consider it art."

"Or classy porn," he rebukes.

That's it. I'm twenty-nine, but where is the maturity in this 33 year-old? He has four years on me. Abruptly, I stand, and he straightens his upper body to ensure we are level, except he is a little taller.

"Not my problem that you can't handle keeping it locked in." My voice rises slightly.

He snickers. "Not my problem you're having a dry spell, which I will assume is the reason that you're a bitter woman."

A sound vibrates under my breath. "Says the man who destroyed my herb garden." I point a finger at him. "Yeah, I'm not buying the whole rabbit overpopulation bullshit."

"Oh, is that not the reason a pile of snow ended up on my driveway right where your sidewalk ends?" His tone is flippant, and he takes an easy sip from his Espresso.

I scoff a sound. "Tell me." I step around the table with my hand on my waist. "Do you use a knife or scissors when you destroy my mail?"

He looks offended, barely. "I would do no such thing for the woman who tips over my recycling bin on garbage day."

"Why do you even bother talking to me? Can't we agree on never saying a word to one another?"

Keats downs the last sip of his espresso. "No can do, Esme. Not until you solve the package situation. I'm a considerate neighbor, but if you'd rather, I could leave your boxes outside your house in the rain or snow. Maybe a squirrel is hungry, too."

I growl, because as much as his ridiculous humor is frustrating, he's right. The last thing I need is camera equipment getting wet. My hands claw my hair because I'm so exhausted from this.

"Clearly, you've cursed my day, and I don't feel like this is the start of the morning that I need, either," he mentions.

We both move in an attempt to walk away, but instead, our feet shuffle, and our effort to step in opposite directions only leads us to the same spot. We both step back, annoyed.

Sighing, I'm debating what to do.

"Have a splendid day. Some of us have to go conquer the world today," he says sarcastically as he begins to walk away.

"With what? Covering for asshole hockey players who cheat?" Shit. Why did I say that? He's going to hound me, and I was saving this information for a rainy day.

Keats stalls and turns sharply back to me. "Say that again?" His voice has a little edge.

A confident and proud smirk spreads on my face. "The photo? I might not have stopped the person who leaked it. In fact, I maybe even helped her pick the right photo."

He closes his eyes for a second, and he seems to be laughing under his breath as he takes in the news, while he shakes his head gently. "Of course you did."

Oliver appears behind him. "You what?"

"Scotty Smith? He cheated."

"And? Why would you care?" Oliver is curious, and he's unreadable.

My eyes run to the side then back at these two men before me. "It was my friend in my photographer group that he lied to. Said he was in the process of a divorce from his wife, while it was clearly not the case. So, a little revenge and one anonymous click on social media seemed only fitting, and I had no problem persuading her to post the photos anonymously. In fact, he can go shove it, considering he wants nothing to do with her and asked her to delete evidence of their weekend getaway a few months back."

It's all spilling out of my mouth, and for some reason, it doesn't feel like the wrong thing to do.

Keats and Oliver look at one another, their faces neutral. But then it happens.

Their faces break, and they laugh, nearly giddy.

I'm puzzled why.

"Thanks for that. Your little activity actually made Oliver and I a lot of money. It's fun when you have extra billable hours." I want to swipe that look of satisfaction off his face. "I mean…" He sets his empty cup on a nearby table. "He kind of had it coming if he cheated, and it did give me a few late hours too many. That little move of yours caused him to no longer be the Spinners' problem and left the door open for a solid player trade."

Oliver sets his hand on Keats's shoulder as his laugh fades off. "I'm going to head to my car. I'll see you at the office. I'm sure your day just got better." He turns to me. "Bye, Esme."

I say nothing but my tipped-up nose tells him goodbye too. But a stabbing set of eyes is still set on me, and back to my morning stare-off with Keats it is.

"Let me guess. You didn't just think it was honorable revenge for your friend, but you also thought it would piss me off one day?"

My lips quirk out, and although, yes, he is right, I sure as hell don't want him to know that. "No. I was just withholding the information and forgot to mention it," I lie.

"Hmm, sure." He isn't buying it. "Listen, as fun as our tit-for-tat is, I need to head to the real world. I would say I'd buy you a coffee, but my instinct to spit in it is probably too high."

I flash him a contrite smile. "Mature of you."

It feels like a minute, but it's probably only a few seconds that we just look at one another. The adrenaline of our conversation still seems to be flowing through me. Did his eyes just dip down to my lips? Or is it me staring at his mouth? Deciding how to tape it shut, of course.

"See ya, neighbor," he rasps.

"What joy."

And with that, he's gone. Now, I have nothing more to hold in my back pocket to piss him off, I guess.

It's a few days later when I return from the gym, and unfortunately, fate would have Keats arriving home at the same time. We seem to park our cars on our respective driveways at the same time.

We both exit our cars with glares on our faces to greet one another. Luckily, we hear the sound of old lady Mrs. Tiller saying hi to us.

She doesn't walk the best, but she's sweet, which is why Keats and I both descend our driveways to meet her on the sidewalk.

"Hi, Mrs. Tiller." I smile. She wants me to call her Sally, but it feels more respectful this way.

Her eyes sparkle at Keats who lost his suit jacket and opted instead for a shirt with the sleeves rolled up. "Look at you. A dashing young man."

"Only for you." He winks at her.

"There is some honesty," I snipe.

Both of them snap their gazes to me.

"You know, you two should come over for tea together. We can play a game of bridge, and you can bring that delicious pie of yours, Esme." She seems excited for the prospect.

Keats places his hand on her shoulder. "That is a lovely idea except I'm not allowed any pie." His cocky look is directed at me, then he rolls his head back to our neighbor. "I'm watching my sugar to stay in shape and all." Oh cute, what a nice cover. What an ass.

"Okay, well, the invite is always there. I need to go home to start my pot roast; the grandkids are coming over."

"Lovely. Do you want me to walk with you?" I offer.

She waves me off. "Don't be silly, dear. I'm still going strong at my young age."

Both Keats and I genuinely smile at her.

"Well, don't be afraid to call out if you need a hero," he jokes with her.

She chuckles and I think nearly fawns over him. But the moment she is far enough away, I shove his shoulder. "Hero? Really? Someone overestimates themselves." And why, oh, why do you need to have a hard, muscled arm?

"Funny. Now if you will excuse me, I need to check my mailbox with hopes that nothing of yours got in there."

I stand tall in a challenge. "What a coincidence, I need to check mine also for the very same reason."

We both almost march to the curb at the end of the driveway, push the flag down, and open the little huts. I grab the envelopes while Keats does the same, and our eyes hold.

In unison we study our mail. A bill, junk mail, and an envelope in handwritten cursive are in my hand. I do a double take when I see Keats examining the very same envelope between his fingers. We seem to be mirroring one another.

Hesitantly, we both open the wax seals, and then I have to smile.

Dear Ms. Jazz,

Your presence is requested at Everhope Manor on Saturday in two weeks to help solve a mystery.

Arrive in character and ready for a delicious dinner that will bring us back in time to the roaring 20s.

I hear Keats laugh as I notice further information about my character, then I step in his direction, closing the space between our boxes to peer at his mail. "You got an invite also?"

"Yep. Who did you get?"

"Lola Jazz, socialite and mistress to Kit Parker." The idea of this is fun, and my smile won't fall. "Who did you get? Detective? A billionaire who survived the Titanic? Is this whole thing Gatsby 20s or Age of Prohibition, like the mob 20s? But really, who did you get?" I list questions.

His grin that erupts is too sinister. Why does he now appear to be Satan with charm?

Keats holds up his invitation that he twists between his two fingers like a playing card. "Well, mistress, looks like you and I are going to be solving a mystery."

The inked name on his invitation is bold enough.

Maybe I should really murder Hailey.

Because standing in front of me is Mr. Kit Parker.

My lover.

4

KEATS

The jazz music sets the mood. As much as I hate the idea of a party that entails dressing in character, I have to give Hailey credit. There is a long center table with high candlesticks and even gold glitter surrounding the place settings, complete with name cards.

"Nice touch with the tucked handkerchief," Oliver mentions as we stand in the corner with drinks in hand, watching guests arrive.

I smirk mid sip, and I must admit that I put in effort. The tux tonight will help fit the part, I guess. "Well, I am Mr. Kit Parker, the party's favorite gangster."

Oliver chuckles. "I heard there's been a murder, and it's a good thing that the detective is here." He tips his hat to me since that's his character.

I hit him with a wry smile. "Does that involve investigating the host?"

He likes that comment. "So be it if Hailey needs a thorough search that might involve no clo—" Oliver stops mid-sentence when he looks over my shoulder and an overdone smile appears. "Liam, my man." Ah, Oliver needs to cover the fact that he has dishonorable intentions for his friend's little sister.

"Hey, guys." Liam arrives and clinks our glasses with his. He's part of our friendship group, working in marketing for the team, but he spends most of his free time with his girlfriend, Ava. "My sister really took this a step too far, but you've got to love it." He grins. "She knows how much Ava loves this stuff. It will be perfect for later."

"Nervous for the big question?" Oliver asks.

Liam beams a smile. "I'm totally ready. The ring's already in my pocket."

I'm happy for him, and he's calm too which is a positive. "Who are you tonight?" I ask.

"Mr. Feathers, a businessman with mafia ties, and Ava is Mrs. Feathers."

We only take brief notice to the new group of people arriving. "What's your character?" he wonders.

Oliver sputters a laugh. "No need to inquire about Mr. Kit Parker; apparently the talk of the town is about his mistress." He clicks his fingers. "Who is playing that role again?" What an ass, which is why I roll my eyes. "Ah yes, none other than Esme. Your favorite human on earth."

The guys let out a deep hearty chuckle. "You know we were all hoping for that. Makes it all the more fun," Liam adds.

"Wonderful. Inflicting misery on me." I'm not enthused, but that's a lie I keep telling myself. And it's only confirmed when I do a double take at the woman entering the dining room.

A short, black sequined flapper dress, long string of pearls, and a feather on her head. Ah, fuck it, the neckline is plunging. I nearly fall back because Esme is both tantalizing and naturally beautiful. Her red lips deserve to be touched with admiration then destroyed by my dick, too.

But it's all the more reason I only let my body tighten for a second before I adjust my shoulders and grimace. Abandoning the guys, I vaguely hear them mumbling. Instead, I catch Esme's eyes in my approach to her, and I can't help but notice that she's eyeing me up and down, with her lashes fluttering in what I would assume is approval.

"Is this what my mistress looks like?" I greet her.

She puffs out a breath and grabs a champagne glass from a passing tray. "Yes. Forgive me if I didn't consult you on my costume choice. Avoiding you the past two weeks felt like the better option." Esme arrived with sass tonight.

"You know, we're in luck. According to the assigned seating, we are sitting at opposite sides of the table."

Her hand finds her heart. "Oh golly, what will I do?"

Stepping closer to her, she doesn't seem to mind. "Behave. I could be the murderer and keen on adding you to my list of victims."

Her brows rise at me. "Don't worry, you murder my soul every time we speak." She seems proud of her little quip.

My tongue darts to the corner of my mouth, and my eyes drift down. I can't help sneaking a small glimpse of her cleavage. But never mind. "Listen, doll, we both know that Liam is popping the question tonight, so shall we be on our best behavior?"

Esme studies me for a second before she juts her chin out. "Fine."

Testing her limits, I reach out to touch her hairband with a feather around her head, but she is quick to swat me away with her gloved hand. "Someone's cranky tonight."

"Cut the crap, Keats. I have no problem throwing this

champagne on you if need be and ending this temporary truce."

I cluck my tongue once before I take a drink. "Nah, the only one wet here is you."

Her entire face flames in one second flat before she pouts. "Bees geez, aren't you something despicable tonight." She throws on the theatrics. I'll give her points for staying in character.

"Shall we both just find our seats at the opposite sides of the table?" I suggest.

"Let's." She pivots in one sharp move and shimmies away, and despite the dim lighting of the room, the outline of her toned legs is clear. Esme really should have thought about adding an inch or two to the hemline. Must everyone nearly see her thighs? One person's stupidity is another person's gain, right?

Everyone takes a few minutes to get settled in their seats. More champagne flows and appetizers are brought. General chitchat is fine, the few times I catch Esme sending me daggers is good, and Hailey hitting her glass with the side of a fork is better. We need to get this show on the road.

"Hello, everyone. This will be such a great night. We will be following our scripts that everyone will be given when we have our main course. But first…" Oh dear god, she has jazz hands. "We will be given some clues, and it will send us on a little scavenger hunt through the manor." She pulls up a letter that looks like it was written on a typewriter. The lady is really into the little details. "It seems our detective" ——she points to Oliver and hands him the note— "comes bearing news that he shall read out."

Oliver gently shakes his head, completely entertained, but since he is a good sport, he's ready to go all in. "It seems that nobody may leave this residence until we find our guilty party. This morning the maid found Mrs. Parker dead in the garden, clearly murdered. Everyone here is a suspect and must find evidence of their innocence. Mr. Porter, the butler, and the head of staff, Ms. Dingle, must search for possible weapons. Mr. Parker would be a prime suspect except it is believed he was with his mistress, Lola Jazz. Therefore, they too will need to search for something that will prove they are innocent."

Esme's eyes blaze open, and internally I'm not surprised by this change to the night's plans.

We're now stuck together.

"Is this for real? Where can we look to speed this up?" Esme trudges along behind me down the hallway.

I stop to turn my attention to her. "Everyone at the table, all twenty of us, have been sent on a scavenger hunt. Just so happens they all get their thrills out of forcing us on this little adventure." An adventure it is, as much as her tits perk up to test me, an hour of listening to her whine isn't ideal either.

"Then let's find a bedroom or something."

My eyes pop out from her bold statement. "Wow, eager. Getting right to business. Really get into character."

She seems to scold herself, and her nose wrinkles. "To find fucking clues. That's what I meant. They're probably in one of the bedrooms or maybe the study."

Between my two fingers I hold up the only clue we've been given that's written on a small card.

Forgotten spaces.

Esme throws her arms up in the air. "What the hell could that mean? Come on, let's go to the study."

She's already strolling past me before I even get a chance

to answer. "My sister will lose it when I tell her about this night. Or rather her boyfriend will."

"I've seen them come over once or twice. I assume you're close," she observes.

"We are."

Esme opens the door to the study filled with dark wood and a leather sofa. "That's nice. I guess you have a piece of heart to spare for some people."

"Silly me for thinking you wanted to have a normal conversation."

She stops, and we face one another. "I'm sorry, okay? This just feels like a little much, you know? Like do we really need an hour to wander the manor before dinner is served promptly at eight with a butler?" It takes a few seconds, but then she realizes that maybe over the top can kind of be fun and a stretched line crosses along her face.

"What's that I see? Is… is that a smile?" I pretend shock.

"Har, har. Now come on, let's search."

Esme instantly heads across the room to fumble with the locked drawers of the grand oak desk, and I peruse the shelf of books, fondly reading the spines. "Quite a collection of law books here."

"That's the thing you notice?"

My eyes swing to her, and I notice the way her fingers softly trail along the smoothness of the desk. "Am I supposed to be noticing something else?"

Her head whips up in my direction with doe eyes; maybe she translates it to something underlying, and judging by the tug on her lips, she seems to enjoy that. "Uh… so law and your sister. The soft attributes of Keats."

I mosey to the desk and land myself on the opposite side then tower over her with my palms planted on the wood.

"Don't worry. I'm anything but soft in other areas," I hiss playfully.

Esme takes a deep breath. "I... will not be imagining that."

Liar.

"How are you so familiar with this place?"

A coy smile breaks out on her face. "I once had a photoshoot here."

"Didn't think this was the place for those kinds of photos."

She lifts her shoulders. "Yeah, well, you can rent out the spaces here. And if you are wondering, it was there." Her finger wiggles, pointing behind me. "Where a woman laid down in nothing but lingerie," she husks.

My lips press together, and I nod slowly. Our eyes strike for a second in a dare. I'm too confident, and I'm the first to move my way to the couch and ceremonially sit down. Esme follows and flops down next to me.

"I don't intend to search this whole building, so let's just go back empty-handed. I doubt anyone would be surprised."

"Agreed," she replies.

"Ooh, look at us agreeing."

She tries to hide her grin but fails. "Champagne does silly things."

Resting my elbow on the back of the smooth maroon leather sofa, I get comfortable. Doesn't seem as though we will be leaving anytime soon, especially when she brings her knees to rest on the cushion, with clearly no plans to scoot away.

I gulp and send a quick memo to my dick to keep it down because Esme is wearing fucking stockings with a garter belt. I know because I get a dangerous glimpse of her upper thigh.

"I'm a gentleman, therefore I shall point out that I can see a hell of a lot of your leg." *Yet not enough.*

Esme appears unfazed and completely satisfied that she's taunting me. "You shouldn't be concerned, since you want to throttle me."

"Fair." Except not adjusting her leg is playing against the rules.

She taps the armrest with the pads of her fingers, maybe trying to come up with a topic to discuss.

"Penny for your thoughts?"

Her grin is sinful. "I'm just remembering how on the very place you're sitting a woman once splayed out her body wearing next to nothing, which I'm sure thrills you."

I ignore her attempts to goad me. "Why did you get into photography?"

Her fingers now play with her long costume pearls. "Easy. There is something heartwarming watching a couple getting engaged and in the bliss of wedding preparation, and boudoir is a celebration of confidence and self-love."

My jaw flexes side to side. "No sarcasm from my end. Those are actually good reasons, honest, too."

"And you? Why law?"

"Easy. I enjoy the fine print of legal proceedings, pushing back when needed, the thrill of closing a deal. Why sports? I grew up in Lake Spark, the Spinners are our pride. Nah, I played hockey in high school, varsity, too."

She snorts a laugh. "For some reason that doesn't surprise me. Were you valedictorian, too?"

I shake my head ruefully. "Actually, no. High school hockey isn't that popular in Illinois unless you go to a private prep school, and that was Lake Spark Academy. The hockey team kind of got away with a lot, including letting grades slip. My studious days were later in college."

"Keats was once a jock. I do like hockey, I admit. Sometimes I even watch it. Growing up in Minnesota, it's a popular sport. You can never go wrong watching hot guys on the ice, either… unless it's you."

A laugh escapes me. "Ah, so is watching hockey like an 'every once in a while, go to a game' kind of thing or 'watch the highlights in the morning from last night's games' kind of thing?"

"Depends on my mood."

"Okay. Your family? I never see them visit."

Maybe a hint of sadness appears. "My parents now live abroad for my dad's work, and my brother is one of those tech people who live in the Silicon Valley bubble. As you know this house was a gift from my great-aunt who didn't have kids, and she chose me. I visited her often, and she always had a warm heart. But family? Yes, on one hand, I know everyone is just a flight away, but on the other, living in my own world is peaceful with no expectations. Just a shame about the neighbors." Esme leans over to nudge my knee. She's being playful, and I'm here for it.

"Sounds like we both are perfectly accepting of life, though."

She shrugs. "I mean, I can't complain. My job is fun, I have friends, like my house, it's not like I'm missing se—"

Ooh, this is too good to pass up.

"Cat got your tongue, doll?"

Her face turns crimson. "Nope." She remains defiant.

Our eyes hold, a hint of ease and an undertone of a smile gracing our lips.

"You're annoying," she reminds me.

Her light facial features don't fade.

She shifts in her seat and a hand sneaks up her opposite leg, but when she leans slightly, she blocks my view as she does something to her dress. Sitting back up, she holds up a flask.

I'm taken aback, surprised yet completely on board with her costume props. "You've been holding out on me. What else are you hiding?"

She pops the top of the silver flask and takes a gulp before she offers it to me. "Age of prohibition and all. I needed to come prepared. Besides, you never know when you'll need a little liquid boost."

I don't hesitate, and I take a swig with no clue what the contents are but relieved when I taste the sting of whiskey.

"You're really unpredictable, huh?" I'm beginning to wonder.

She snatches the flask back. "And you are a little less uptight when you're in costume as a gangster. How does it feel to be on the other side of the law?"

The corners of my mouth twist. "There is nothing wrong with being career driven and damn good at your job."

She snickers. "See? You need to check your work-life balance. I've heard that line way too many times since I've moved to Everhope Road. It's kind of depressing."

I watch her take one more sip before she twists the cap closed and takes zero notice of me as she tucks the item back up under her dress. So be it, I try to peer over her arm for a glimpse.

"A truce, remember?" I remind her.

She grins over her shoulder at me. "Just stating facts. It's not a jab."

"Fine. You shouldn't flash your leg, it isn't proper." I kind of just said that to cause her to give me side-eye. It's fun.

"You've seen more. I'm supposed to be your mistress, remember?" she counters with her brows raised.

Just then the door bursts open with a giggly woman clinging to a man.

"Oh shit, sorry." Hailey stumbles back out, and my head tips to see that Oliver is draped around her.

The door shuts, and Esme looks at me with mutual interest. "They are totally tipsy," she comments.

I interject, "Or intent on destroying this couch for other activities."

We both laugh because we're on the same page for that.

A warm silence forms around us, except this time it's calming.

"Should we actually search for this clue?" she suggests almost reluctantly.

I blow out a breath. "Probably. What in the world is a forgotten place that isn't a sexual reference? Is there a hidden closet or something?"

Her finger pops up. "A hidden bookcase?"

We both make our way to examine the books, even pull out a few, but nothing. I scratch my jaw, no longer in the mood for the game.

"Isn't the whole point of being a lawyer searching for clues and solving them? Discovery or something like that?"

I look at her, impressed. "Wow, someone is throwing out legal terms."

She flashes her eyes at me. "I'm full of surprises."

My eyes narrow as I watch her read the spines of the books. Her fingers crawl along the titles, and her half smile floats. She's an image of Alice in Wonderland with more skin showing.

"Got it." She snaps her fingers, breaking me from her spell. Before I can process, she rushes back to the sofa and her hand dives between the cushions. "Voila. Everyone forgets about the cracks in the sofa." Esme pulls up a white handkerchief with a lipstick stain and a small notecard.

This is your clue to bring back to dinner. Evidence left behind from your morning endeavors.

"Really?" My voice squeaks. "Kit Parker and Lola Jazz decided to use the study? Classy." A suave grin hits me.

"Ugh, now we can move on. I'm hungry," Esme whines.

I reach for the handkerchief, but she keeps her grip tight. "What? I'll put it in my inner pocket with my cigars."

"Cigars? You really went all in for this."

"Really? I'm not the one carrying around a flask between her thighs."

Her face remains steady. "I can hold the evidence just fine."

"Just give it to me." I manage to clasp the end of the cloth.

But she yanks it away. "No." She wins, and she's already tucking it near her tits under a strap.

"Aren't we a little jezebel tonight."

"I am, because I might not have mentioned yet that by accident, I hit your mailbox earlier when I returned home," she casually throws out.

My face falls. "What?"

Esme shrugs and holds her hands up in defense. "I just wasn't paying attention when I got home earlier from a shoot. I was hoping to inform you tomorrow when we are probably all hungover."

I gripe and begin to lead us out. "You really have zero respect for my property. So inconsiderate." Now I'm getting boiled again.

"I'm not sorry. You deserve it."

My nose tips up. "Did you just say that you're not sorry?"

"Yes, Mr. Respect for Property. The man who for sure destroys some of my boxes just to piss me off."

Well, that several minutes of peace just went out the door.

We walk down the hall bickering again. "Then don't fucking have the boxes delivered to my house."

"Message has been clear from the get-go. Geesh, I don't even get this cranky when your stupid newspaper ends up on my lawn. And who the hell still has newspapers delivered?"

I hold my finger up, ready to school the hell out of this woman. "First, the former owner had a lifetime subscription and forgot to end it. Secondly, it's the Sunday paper, including financial news, and that accompanies my morning coffee perfectly."

Esme snorts a sound and bites her inner cheek. "Stealing and boring. Sounds about right."

We continue to pace down the hall in our frenzy of arguing. "Excuse me for staying up to date on world events, and darling, boring is the one thing I am not. Besides, even if I was, it's the boring ones who normally harbor a wild side in other areas."

Her hands form fists by her sides. "Can you not just let me have one enjoyable night where I don't need to think about the way you probably chain someone to your bed?"

"No! You're my mistress." My voice rises an octave while I rile her.

She glimpses sidelong at me as we continue to walk. "Only in a fictional world, because in reality, I would have to be insane."

"I'm so relieved you're sitting on the other side of the table, because I swear you don't want me with a fork near you right now."

"Uh, actually, the seating arrangements changed," Hailey interjects awkwardly.

Apparently, in our fury, we didn't realize we made it back to the dining room, making a scene.

"No. Nope. Not a good idea," Esme reiterates my own thoughts.

Hailey gives us a pointed look and tilts her head in her brother's direction. Shit. The proposal. That's why musical chairs happened.

I'm going to have to suck this up.

"I KNEW IT WAS YOU. What better way to ask you to be my wife than with candles all around and your favorite theme." Liam and Ava are at the head of the table. She's already crying, and Liam could use improvement on his proposal. The ring box appears and opens, and the woman is in shock, except I know she's been calculating this for months, but I'll give her points for her acting skills. "Will you be my Mrs. Feathers?"

The immediate titter causes my head to turn to Esme sitting to my right. She's desperately trying to keep her chortle in with her hand over her mouth. Rightfully so, because what in the world is my man Liam doing with this cheesy proposal?

"Yes, I'll be your Mrs. Feathers. You're my favorite man with mafia ties," Ava responds spiritedly.

Esme sputters again, and her face flushes; she is about to burst.

Feral instinct kicks in. I scoop my hand under the table and find her naked thigh between the straps of her stockings, then I claw into her flesh in an attempt to settle her down. Leaning in close to her ear, my nose scraping the edge of her face with silky skin, I open my mouth. "Get. It. Together," I grit out in a low voice.

She instantly stalls, and her breath hitches. My guess is it's due to the fact that I press harder into her skin, not so accidentally sliding up half a finger in length. It's either the alcohol or the heat from the thousands of candles, but this woman is warm and soft between her legs. I'm nowhere near her core, but I sense I've done something to her. My sixth sense.

Fingers on her thigh seems to do the trick because her hysterics disperse into oblivion, or maybe she just has a nocturnal enjoyment to respond to my touch. She gulps a breath and attempts to smile like the rest of the room at the newly engaged couple.

Why the hell isn't she reaching under the table to push my hand away?

We don't look at one another, not even when my hand abandons her leg when we all begin to clap. In fact, I casually pick up my wine glass for a sip, as though I didn't just touch her in a way that can still her into quiet.

She smiles tightly as everyone has elation written on their faces, and in the process of celebration, she accidentally knocks her fork to the ground. Her shoulder bumps against mine as she leans down to pick it up. Just as I'm enjoying the view of her long back, a sharp sting hits near my ankle and slowly slides up.

The little vixen is using the fork on me, causing me to clear my throat and my body to tense and equally enjoy her little game.

Esme continues to look forward, not giving me a single glance as the fork rakes up my leg with just enough pressure to be gentle yet firm. "Oh, phonus balonus, I'm such a klutz, dropping things, but I think… I found the fork."

No. This is bad.

That fork can absolutely not go any higher.

…and it does.

She stops mid-thigh, my blood burning through my entire body.

"Must be all dirty now. I better stick to sipping champagne and sucking olives." My eyes pop out when she glances over her shoulder with a sly smile.

The guy across from us looks at us strangely but then turns to the guest at his side.

"Well, don't forget to swallow," I mutter out.

Her eyes gawk at my boldness. I get the upper hand when I discreetly rip her hand away from my leg, dropping her wrist to the side as she claws the utensil.

I should stand, leave, and get some air. Cool down.

But I'm a damn professional at playing it neutral.

So, I remain seated and watch as the murder mystery continues. Luckily there is some story audio on an app, as our script drags forever. It's a true amateur play happening, a throwback to my sixth-grade drama club. Between food and bad gangster accents, it wasn't until the end when it turned out my fictional wife was having an affair with the driver, and he'd killed her with poison.

What a shocker.

Time to wrap this up and get home. Apparently, I have a mailbox to fix in the morning.

"You're okay to drive? Otherwise, I can order you two a cab," Hailey checks in like the super organizer she is, as we're all standing at the bottom of the grand staircase.

"I'm fine. I stopped drinking by the third course. Or did I just zone out? I'm not sure. Anyhow, I only had a drink earlier and wine with dinner."

She smiles in agreement. "Perfect. You can take Esme home too. She arrived with a friend of mine because they needed to pick up extra supplies at the store."

Esme looks between us. "Or not."

Hailey has a crooked grin. "You live next door to one another."

"And? Oliver lives down the street," Esme highlights.

I smile tightly. "Let me guess. He's helping you clean up?" I ask Hailey.

"Well, I… maybe." Her voice is uneven.

Rubbing the back of my neck, I accept the cards we've been dealt. "Fine."

"No," Esme shoots out.

I must appear annoyed with everyone, and I'm happy to get the message across. "Don't be ridiculous or I'll throw you over my shoulder. So be a doll and get in the damn car."

Esme's jaw hangs low, and Hailey just leaves us with a giggle under her breath.

"I'm only doing this because I care about the planet, so carpooling it is," she justifies her willingness to appease.

"Touching. Now come on."

A long silence hits us when we get into my car. Even when I rev up the engine which causes her to huff, she refrains from speaking. Only two minutes later with her perfume now sticking to my car interior does she dip her toes into conversation.

"That was a well-planned evening."

I focus on the road. There have been foxes spotted along the road at night recently. "A shame one guest decided to be wildly rude during the marriage proposal."

"Oh, come on. Did you not hear that? You must have been laughing inside too."

"But I didn't let the world know it."

Esme shakes her head and stares out the window. The damn dashboard light glows on her silky thighs, and her dress's black sequins glint a sparkle.

"I still hate this car, even if the seat has heating and the leather is smooth and nice against the skin," she comments as she slides her hand along the side panel.

"Speaking of skin, way to go with the costume, by the way. Plan on joining a strip club?"

She sneers at my sentence. "Rude as always," she points out. "Why wasn't there bootleg alcohol or moonshine tonight? It's the age of prohibition, right? I mean, it would help my agitation right now."

I keep my hands on the steering wheel; whatever I do, safety first.

"Having my fingers on your thigh seemed to calm you." Okay, so I can't help myself.

Why has she grown quiet? And why are her fingertips now twirling her necklace near her cleavage.

Is she actually trying to toy with me?

"Cat got your tongue, doll?"

"Call me doll one more time and I swear I'll use a fork differently next time…"

She can't finish her sentence, which is fine, as I'm now pulling up my driveway.

"Your chariot has brought you to your destination."

Her lips pop. "Okay."

Neither one of us moves when I turn the engine off.

I tap the wheel, patiently waiting for either one of us to end this boiling pot otherwise known as my car.

Another second goes by.

And another.

My head against the headrest rolls to the side to look at

the woman of my contempt, and Esme seems to mirror my move until our eyes pin one another.

"Want to come inside for a nightcap?" I coolly offer as adrenaline seems to be kicking in.

Instantly she gasps. "Yes."

5
ESME

Our steps feel heavy yet not terrifying.
In fact, dare I say exciting?
Why? It's just a nightcap. He seems like a man with a good whiskey collection. It's probably on a tray in his living room with those crystal tumblers.

"Whiskey? Your flask must be out, or rather I noticed you threw it in your purse when we left."

The corners of my mouth lift up as it seems my theory about his drink of choice is correct. "Yeah, sounds good."

We step up to his porch as if this is a normal occurrence. Then again, nothing about tonight has been usual. I'm off balance from the enjoyment of being stuck at a murder mystery with him.

I watch as he unlocks the door then turns off the alarm. I shiver which causes me to cross my arms over my body and my dress that I can confidently say looks sexy and perfect on me.

I hate to think it, but seeing Keats dressed like a character from the Gatsby era is distressing… it's sexy. His hair slicked back and the way his eyes narrow in on his fictitious mistress have been melting my insides all evening. Only made worse by his fingers digging into my thigh and cross-wiring my body. He's bold.

The door clicks closed behind us, and I follow him. When he flicks the lights on, I quickly observe my surroundings. This may be an old house, but inside, it's anything but. Completely refurbished and updated. However, screw the house, because the vision of Keats tossing his bow tie to the side, not a care where it lands, and his fingers popping open the top buttons of his shirt is by far a better view.

A strong knot in the center of my body is weighing me down but screaming for this heightened moment to end.

We haven't said anything, and the moment Keats turns around, we both know why.

There is no intention for a drink.

For two people who can't stand one another, we move in unison damn well.

Lunging for one another, our mouths meet for a harsh kiss. His arm encircles my body, and in one jolt, glues my body to his. I'm not protesting. Not when our lips angle for more and not when our tongues meet for a thrashing. My hands come up to curl around his shirt next to the freed buttons. I'm not sure I can stand otherwise.

We're an inferno of two people who are desperate not to question this and just keep moving our hands, continuing our punishing kisses.

Even in the brief pause as we gasp for air with our panting breaths and our eyes meet for a second, we still both silently agree that this isn't going to stop. We confirm it with our hands wandering and my fingers eagerly working down his shirt to get the damn buttons undone.

His palms on my ass are firm and frustrating because I want them there, and up, and down, everywhere.

Our mouths can't part, and our movements are fierce. We're so out of control that we begin to circle and stumble to a direction unknown. Without breaking our hungry kiss, he slides his open shirt down his arms, littering the floor. We continue to spin until the sound of a thud and furniture hitting behind my knees causes us to stop.

Suddenly, I feel a cool surface against my back after I'm hoisted up in one move and set on the side table by the front door. Did we really not make it further into his house before we combusted?

We paw at one another, and my lips feel swollen, but I don't stop. I can't. A hand yanks my necklace, and the beads scatter across the floor, the sound of pearls bouncing not deterring us. I don't even know whose fault it is because every part of us is exploring in haste.

Keats murmurs a sound against my skin, and his teeth scrape along my neck as his lips draw a line down. A sizzling tingle spreads through me in a tidal wave causing my nipples to turn to hard nubs. My dress is bunched at my middle, and I purr when I feel the flick of a garter strap against my thigh due to Keats's finger, and the growl in my ear admits his crime.

We're in luck that my underwear isn't attached to the garter belt, otherwise we would have to slow down to pop every latch. Instead, I can instantly drag my legs up his thighs until they wrap around his waist to press our bodies tightly.

His hot breath does something to me. My skin prickles and an unknown realm that's exciting in a different way than I was expecting hits me, tightening in my core but blossoming everywhere else. It's making me impatient.

Our heavy breathing fills my ears, and I like Keats this way. Quiet because his mouth is trailing a circle around my cleavage due to the straps of my dress and bra hanging halfway down my arm. There are only a few inches between us, but I close the space by yanking on his belt, bringing him closer.

My breasts are not abandoned as he kisses over the lace, grazing one nipple with his lips while he slides the bottom of my dress up and caresses my thighs.

Then it happens.

At last, our eyes connect with acknowledgment that we're crossing lines, and the only answer we give is silence. Instead, we don't blink as the back of his fingertips tease me as they feather up my thighs.

I whimper, and his cunning smirk begins to form. Swallowing, I feel my clit pulsing and my hips buck up, wanting his touch. Keats has no qualms about walking his fingers up slowly, causing agony for me, keeping my eyes a prisoner in the process. The moment his finger hooks under the waistband of my thong, he smirks because he's the devil.

And I want him everywhere and inside of me.

"I knew it." He begins to pull the fabric down roughly, stepping back to slide the fabric off my legs, the heels and stockings still on my feet. But the other item is tossed to the side.

"I don't care about your theories, just don't stop."

His hand snakes around to the back of my head to bring my forehead to his. It's gruff and not delicate, and I love it. "Open your legs wide, Esme." His tone is sharp and demanding.

Obeying, I wait with zero patience for him to give me the slightest relief.

Keats swipes his finger along my pussy and instantly I moan, and he hisses. "You're a naughty girl. For someone who hates me, you seem eager for my cock."

"Shut the fuck up, Keats," I rasp.

I tug at his pants, and when they lower enough, I shove my hand between us to cup his hard boxer-brief-covered cock. My head falls back because I discover that he's just as big as his ego, and I can't complain about that.

"I'm going to enjoy making you speechless with my cock inside you."

He quickly searches for something and then spots his suit coat on a nearby hook, with one hand he dips into the pocket to pull out his wallet and grabs a condom, ripping it open with his teeth. I need him to hurry up.

It happens so fast, but I feel Keats inching inside of me, deeper, then some more.

We moan in sync, adjusting to the new sensation. Our bodies are connected, and our lips dance before they slam together for a kiss. His thrusts begin to pick up, and I rest my hands on his shoulders, clawing my nails into him. I'm holding on for dear life because he hits me deep on every pump, exactly where I like it.

The table is shaking, and my ankles cross behind his thighs to keep us snug. Both bra straps falling to my elbows without any of our effort brings new opportunity for sensations to overload inside of me. Keats wastes no time and dips his mouth down and harshly bites the bottom of my throat near my collarbone. A long moan escapes me because the tip of his pointed tongue swirls down to my covered nipple causing an overbearing sensation.

He's making me wild. Uninhibited and frantic. Keats grunts when I tighten my pussy around his length, and my slick heat keeps him tightly enveloped inside of me.

"I found a redeemable quality about you," he breathes out as he fucks me mercilessly.

The only way I can answer is with a pleasured whine because he moves to my other nipple and his teeth nibble, then he opens his mouth to speak. "Your pussy feels fantastic around my cock."

"Don't stop. Just…" I writhe again, unable to form words.

That's fine too because I prefer biting into his neck as our speed increases.

"Keats." It spills out of my mouth because his finger slipped between us to rub my clit. I'm so damn close, and I'm getting dizzy.

I can't help it and look between us to see where we're connected. The condom is glistening from my desire for him.

"You like the view?" he whispers into my hair.

"Your cock seems to be your best quality."

He laughs under his breath and circles with a new pace around my clit. My body wants it too much.

"I'm going to…" I begin to convulse all over his cock, and my body shudders and a slur of curses comes out of my mouth.

"Fuck, that feels good." His labored breath hints that he is close, and when my shaking begins to subside, he changes his rhythm, and not long after, he too comes undone.

Damn it.

This was better than I wanted it to be.

I just needed to work out some issues. I wasn't expecting Keats to take me hard and for me to enjoy every second. Or wanting his mouth in other places or having the image of me riding him seared into my brain.

Keats stays inside me as we both slowly fall back to earth, with what we did now disappearing into the clouds that circle around us.

We nuzzle our noses for a brief second, one last touch that's a slither of tender understanding, because we don't need words to express that we maybe chipped away at our hostilities. Only maybe.

But the moment is brief. Keats pulls out of me and adjusts his shoulders as he takes a moment to gather himself. He studies me, and I'm completely destroyed, my hair a mess and my dress disheveled. The smirk that crawls on his mouth doesn't feel vicious, it's admiration, and I'm not sure it's for his ability to deliver either. Instead, he is soaking me in, and it doesn't calm the thunder roaring through my chest.

It's only for a second or two because his eyes then abandon me, because like me, he realizes the predicament we just found ourselves in.

My lips quirk out, contemplating what the next move is.

But my mouth stretches to one side because he's spent and recovering after he came as hard as I did.

"I need to get rid of this," he says, his eyes squeezing shut as he takes an audible breath, then his eyes pop open to glare at me with uncertainty.

Hopping off the table, I slip a bra strap up my arm. "And I won't be here when you return."

I debate finding my thong, but I would rather escape at the speed of light. Literally, we just went at it like wild animals, and it didn't even take a debate.

"Yeah, sure." He sounds drowsy.

When he walks away, I sigh and quickly make my escape.

Outside, the cool air shocks me into reality.

That did not just happen.

But it did.

And the scary part is that we may aggravate one another to no end, but that doesn't seem to be the case once our clothes come off.

KEATS

I'm hungover.

Not from alcohol but *her*.

I have claw marks on my back to make sure I don't forget, either.

What transpired last night was perhaps needed. Maybe it will calm our constant conflict.

But fuck. Esme felt perfect around my cock. And her afterglow due to me was… breathtakingly beautiful.

And now what the hell do I say to her?

I have to think quickly because as I walk down my driveway to collect my Sunday paper—from the mailbox, not damaged because she was egging me on—my not-so-impeccable timing causes me to see from the corner of my eye Esme is exiting her house in yoga pants with a rolled mat tucked under her arm.

She's fumbling with her keys and dives into her bag for something, and she pulls out her sunglasses. It's then when she peers up and faces me that her rush subsides.

We both stall for a long second, surveying the other and deciding how to act.

"Morning," I greet her.

Her eyes snap open, nearly startled, before she inhales a deep breath. "Uh, I'm expecting a package later this week. I triple-checked the address situation and it should be fine."

Is she nervous or just plain rude for no good morning?

I scratch my cheek. "Great. I'm not sure I will be home much, anyhow."

Hey eyes widen slightly. "Oh?"

That's what you moaned last night.

"Late work week ahead. The team is preparing for the draft and need to be ready to have contracts good to go for signatures."

Her head jostles softly side to side. "Of course, that makes sense."

Now, we are both trying to avoid making eye contact. I rock on my heels, but then realize that acting as though nothing happened is probably what is best. I don't need an awkward morning after. That's what happens with other women. They're eager for me to promise them a romantic dinner or another night together. But Esme? The woman who is standing before me with doe eyes and disdain probably buried deep within? Well, she might be my golden ticket to physical gratification.

She holds her keys up. "Yoga class. I'm going to be late," she mentions and begins to turn her feet.

"Have fun. Oh…" I snap my fingers. "I just assumed the fake pearls could get tossed." I don't mean to bring last night up. It doesn't even cross my mind, but a logistic popped into my head.

Now Esme is hurrying into the driver's seat. "Yeah, sure." She slams her door shut before I can reply, even though I have no clue what words would tumble out anyhow.

Or if I should even bring up that she left her thong at my

place. It was destroyed the way her pussy craved me, which is why the fabric found its way to my garbage can. Even though I would probably have fun stuffing it into her mouth.

I wince as she backs her car up in a far-too-fast speed, and she's on her merry way.

Combing a hand through my hair, a long exhale passes through my lips.

Running into one another after destroying my front hall table: Check.

The box of bagels sitting on my kitchen counter are appealing. I'm starving, and maybe I need to stock up on some carbs after ramming into my neighbor until we both came.

I slide the European-sized mug for coffee under my state-of-the-art coffee machine. It's confusing as hell which buttons to use, which is why I normally stop by Foxy Rox in the morning, but my at-home coffee is still a good brew.

"Here." I motion to Oliver sitting at the counter.

"Thanks. My head is kind of slow today. I keep forgetting to remind myself that drinking in our 30s is not the same as our 20s." He brings the rim of the mug to his lips.

I chuckle at that fact as I open the box for an onion bagel. "What was the deal with Hailey last night?"

Oliver scoffs. "Nothing, man, we just joked around."

"Not going to make your move?"

He laughs at me. "And have Liam murder me? Nah."

Pressing my lips out, I consider his plan, and my doubts he will hold strong remain. "Okay, so a quick breakfast and caffeine fix and then we can go over which docs we will divvy out for this week's workload."

Oliver's growing smirk concerns me, even more so when he slips his hand into his pocket only to pull out a little pearl bead that he holds between his fingers. "Found this in your hall when I came in."

Damn. Must have missed one. Then again, that necklace was demolished in our fucking endeavors.

Casually, I step toward my coffee machine to make another cup for myself. "Did you?"

"Something you want to share?"

"Not particularly." I push a button, and the sound of beans grinding calms me every single time.

"It's okay to say that you had a guest over last night. I won't judge you if it is your favorite neighbor either." He sounds pleased with himself.

My fingers clasp onto the cup, and when the last drop falls, I bring the rim to my mouth. "So what? We got out a little aggression."

He slams his hand onto the counter and seems ecstatic. "I knew it! Eventually, you two needed to work out whatever vibe you have going."

"Vibe?" My brows rise.

He looks at me like I'm crazy. "Everyone knows that bickering is a front for deeper intentions."

I shake my head gently side to side. "Well, it happened, and that is that. We ran into one another earlier as if it is a normal day."

"Really?" His nose wiggles. "Huh."

"The only thing to come out of it is perhaps a period of calm for the coming weeks. A temporary ceasefire in our intent on wanting to kill one another."

Oliver seems doubtful. "But is it, though? Angry sex does things to people. So good luck with your idea."

My exhausted breath can be heard. "Can we just focus on

why you came over?"

"Came over? My guess is that it isn't the same as the way you came with her."

"You're a little crass this morning." I throw him a pointed look.

He shrugs. "What? This news makes my day. I want to see this all unravel. I mean, how the hell do you live next to the woman you had meaningless sex with?"

My jaw slides to the side. Huh, I didn't think about that. "It will be fine." Or maybe not.

"Sure. Make that your motto."

"I regret telling you anything."

"Then clean up the evidence a little better," he counters.

I raise my palm to indicate for him to tune down this conversation. "Seriously, can we now focus on work?"

"We have that work event coming up. Are you bringing a date?"

"No," I instantly reply.

Oliver gives me an *oh really* look. "I'm off the hook, as I'm our representative for that conference out in Anaheim. You're the one who should probably not arrive solo, and you might have a solution for that."

Tightening my jaw, I can't even process anything anymore. "Work," I direct.

Oliver reluctantly agrees, giving me an opportunity to be distracted for a few hours.

IT'S dinnertime when I get home. Normally, I'm not back this early on a workday, or when the sun is hanging low, but I headed into the office at the crack of dawn. Parking, I see the handyman packing up his truck across the street. They've been working on that house forever.

Walking up the few steps to my porch, I rub my face and groan instantly.

Seriously? A box the size of half my body? This is what the delivery man has left me as a gift that keeps on giving? I tilt my head to read the label. Yep. It's Esme Pines. My little demon.

Purely because it's been a long day, my annoyance scale has tipped to one side and not in her favor.

Opening my front door quickly, I set my laptop bag inside then shut the door. Luckily, I already rolled up my sleeves and got rid of the tie in the car. Carrying the box, I at least get a little arm workout.

Balancing the box as I make my way to Esme's front door, I wonder how she would even lift this thing?

Setting it down again, I knock on Esme's door. Sure, the doorbell would work, but that is far too elegant for my building fury right now. A strong fist against the wood of her door is by far better.

I hear her grumbling something, and she seems to get the message to powerwalk. She peeks through the glass next to the door and immediately her shoulders sag.

When she opens the door, her glare is a reminder that we are capable of forgetting the other night.

Except...

She looks hot with her hair up in a knot on the top of her head, her tight tank pushing up her tits, and her flower skirt showing off her knees. Being easy on the eyes is not new. But having been inside of her? Well, I think my attraction level just went into a different realm.

"Yes?" Esme's hip tips out and her arm rests above her head on the door pane.

"Ah, there is my sassy little demon." I give her a fake smile then tap the box with my foot. "How the hell is this still happening?" My demeanor changes.

Her face falls. "Again? No."

"Did you not see this thing sitting on my porch? Couldn't have taken it away?"

That glare of hers is like an arrow to my dick. "Excuse me for not crossing private property, and no, I didn't see it."

"Here. It's yours."

I notice her eyes drop down, and she bites her bottom lip. A few reangles of her head and I realize she is trying to figure out how to get this beast into her house.

A groan leaves me, and I lean down because there is no way she could move this, to be honest. "Where does it go?"

"You don't need to—"

"Don't fucking argue while I have whatever the hell this is in my arms."

She opens the door wide open. "Upstairs to the right."

Scurrying past her, I move quickly, as this box isn't the lightest. Finally, when I set it down upstairs, I take a moment and realize I'm inside her house. I've never been here.

Where am I exactly? "What is this place?"

There is a bed with old-fashioned bars at the headboard, and it's simple. Camera equipment is stored in the corner. Something about this room doesn't feel like your average guest room.

"This room is for photoshoots."

Ah.

"And in the box?"

She clears her throat. "A new pouf for the end of the bed."

I squeeze the bridge of my nose. "Humor me. What is that needed for?"

Esme licks her lips that begin to slyly stretch. "A place where women can sit… in lingerie."

I kind of want specifics but display that I'm unaffected, rolling my eyes. "How is that riveting news?"

"Maybe because your mind hasn't yet imagined in what position she's sitting." That sultry voice of hers, I want to punish her for it.

Stepping closer to her, I grimace. "Aren't you cute."

She glances away for a quick second then back to me, feeling satisfied with herself. "Thank you for carrying the box. See? I have manners." Her eyes seem to be challenging me, inviting me.

Surveying her, I take one determined step, causing her breath to catch. "I'm not sure words are enough."

This is escalating quickly, and I don't give a damn.

A flicker in her eyes and the way her body changes stance instantly snaps the air in the room. My hand comes up and I cup her jaw with a little force, causing her eyes to tie with my own.

"Which one of us is going on their knees? Because I'm the one who really has manners tonight," I rasp with my thumb dragging her bottom lip side to side.

She swallows. "Isn't the answer clear? I'm supposed to be thanking you." This woman's sensual voice is her curse, and I want to cause her to beg.

Dropping to my knees, I slowly reach under her skirt, with my eyes arrowing straight into her. "I want you to suffer."

Her breath grows heavy, and I feel her fingers rake through my hair.

The moment she steps out of her lace panties, my lips are placing kisses up her calves and then I switch to my mouth skimming up her inner thigh.

"How is this not in my favor?" she wonders in a breathy voice.

I snicker against her skin. "Because once my tongue is on you, then you'll never have it better."

Up, up, and then I'm there.

The apex of her thighs, her scent hitting my nose and my center of gravity easing. My tongue darts out and circles her skin, but I don't give her what she wants, and she tries to hide her pout.

"I want to taste you," I admit my impatience in a whisper that wasn't supposed to be heard.

Esme begins to tilt her hips forward as if she can bring her pussy to my lips.

"On the floor," I murmur into her skin.

No reluctance, she kneels down with her eyes still stabbing my own. She lies back on the hardwood and rests on her elbows, with her legs parted and her feet firmly planted.

I have no intention of stopping on this road. I'm on knees then my stomach and make her whimper the moment my tongue makes contact with her wet pussy, and her taste could be my dessert every day.

Her moan encourages me, and I lap her up a few strokes before I explore her clit.

"Fuck, Keats."

My eyes shift up while I continue to work her. Esme's head falls back as she hums a sound. I want her completely naked, but that's not what this is.

Dipping my tongue inside of her brings her writhing underneath me. Her face is flushed when she peers down at me with her one hand fisting my hair. I know that I'm doing something right as her hips slant up and she begins to ride my mouth.

"I think I want to be punished more by you," she softly cries out.

Pausing on her pussy, I give her one more lash against her swollen nub then abandon her.

"You might regret saying those words one day," I playfully warn her.

"Let's not debate this. Please make me come," she pleads.

I grin in pride. "Esme, your pussy has to wait. It doesn't deserve a quick release. And as much as your mouth needs to be stuffed with my cock, fucking your pussy is what I want because it's a good way to destress from my day at the office."

Hovering over her, I hold my weight on one arm, nudge her arms against the rug above her splayed body, and jam two of my free fingers into her mouth, catching her off guard.

"I bet this mouth can handle it." She nods, and I add another finger, her eyes mesmerized on me. "Your mouth likes to be filthy." I'm not asking, I'm telling her as her mouth salivates and she begins to suck. "My little demon is eager."

Popping my fingers out, I grip her chin and slant my mouth over hers but not touching. I squeeze her jaw and her lips part open, purposely allowing my spit to slowly fall from my mouth to land in her own. "And a dirty girl, too," I whisper.

One kiss. That's all she gets.

She feels desperate to kiss me harder, and I only reward her with my mouth capturing her bottom lip for a nip.

After all, she's submitting to everything I'm doing.

Dropping my touch from her jaw, her swollen lips that are my doing look natural on her, the rose on her cheeks too. Sliding down her body, I push her thighs apart with not an ounce of gentleness, and I quickly unbuckle, unzip, and pull down my pants just enough. It happens so fast, yet I still appreciate the way her arms stretch out, attempting to touch me in awe. I'm cocky that way to assume it's that.

"Keats." My name trailing out of her mouth in a labored breath is making me eager to slam into her.

"Is this what you want? To be filled up?"

Her body thrashes and twists, struggling to bring my tip closer to her pussy. "Yes," she gasps.

"That's a good girl. Begging." There must be a glint in my eye that translates to a warning.

"If my begging is to your fucking standards then hurry up," she replies in a playful clipped voice.

Aligning to her entrance, I nudge in. We moan together in the instant feel of one another, her pussy tight around my cock.

I begin to move, working my way up to being relentless in my pursuit to make us come.

Her nails. Why do they feel so damn perfect when she claws into my shirt? She's attempting to imprint on me like a wild wolf.

There is no doubt in my mind that she might be sore tomorrow as we continue to fuck roughly on the floor.

I'm not sure who is grunting and who is moaning, who is thrusting harder, because she's clenching around me and moving to accompany every plunge in and out.

We get there. A mind-blowing, coming undone, will-struggle-to-recover orgasm.

Esme wails, and I roar out my release shortly after as we grind against one another.

It takes half a minute before we sink onto the floor to come down until I end up as a starfish on my back, and her knees remain pointed to the ceiling with her thighs splayed out and her skirt bunched around her waist. We both wait for our breaths to even out.

She felt so damn good, the room is spinning.

On the outside, I may have control of her, but inside, I'm unhinged around her.

Then it dawns on me.

"Condom." My tone is flat because I'm still trying to lower my heart rate.

"Pill. As much as you're an ass, I know you're not that much of one."

My face puzzles as I continue to stare at the ceiling. "That's a lot of trust."

She shimmies her skirt back down. "Regardless of what we may think of one another, we're not that far off the crazy wagon."

I let it go because she's right. Under our barbs, we don't really think the other is a bad person. We are annoyance.

Continuing our deflation of the last ten minutes, we say nothing. But she finally opens her mouth and in a plain tone asks, "Pizza?"

"Sure."

"Good. Because the pizza that I ordered before your arrival should be here any minute, and I need you to open the door while I clean up."

I smile, but she can't see it. "Ah, you need my services. Give me a second."

Which means that neither one of us is storming off like last time.

ESME

Splashing water onto my face, it doesn't help get rid of the flush in my body. In the mirror, I face my own astonishment.

Keats and I did it again.

This time, he had me in a trance that keyed into my inner inhibitions. Shamelessly, I submitted to him without much persuasion needed. Every little thing intrigued me, and I wanted more.

Cleaning up, I scold myself internally that we let the moment get between us, though I don't regret it.

It's when my feet land at the bottom of the stairs and the smell of pizza fills the air that I straighten my shoulders and take a deep breath. How are we going to play this?

Walking through the living room to the kitchen, I find Keats opening the box and then his gaze lifts up.

"Look at us being cordial and sharing a pizza."

It causes a short laugh to leave my mouth. "Or I just need carbs and think irrationally when in this state."

His sexy mouth smirks. The mouth that tastes of me, and the mere thought causes my pussy to pulse.

"You are a BBQ sauce on pizza kind of gal, I see."

Shrugging, I approach the counter. "With shredded chicken, onion, and maybe some corn and pineapple, it's perfect."

"Respect."

Our eyes linger for a few ticks, and it makes me nervous but not in a negative way; it's the I'm-afraid-I'm-blushing way. "Plates?"

"Not sure they're needed after I just fucked the snark out of you," he deadpans.

A warm wry smile spreads on my lips. "What a Keats thing to say."

To my surprise, he doesn't say anything and instead turns the box to offer me a slice.

"Your pictures?" He tips his head up to the wall behind me near the window.

Fondly, I smile. "Yeah, memories really. My Labrador dog growing up. Family from the rare times we spend holidays together. Places I love. I did a whole photography trip around Maine two years ago. That's what photos are for; to trap memories in a frame. It's like a cage of stilled time."

"That's... a good way of looking at it. Does that mean you keep pictures of your ex somewhere here?"

That entertains me. "Hell no. We ended like a year and a half ago. He wasn't very good in certain departments." I wince. Nor was it exciting to see one another even for dinner. I mean, he was a nice guy, just not riveting, and it was a short-lived relationship.

Keats huffs a laugh. "Wow. You have my admiration for being honest about that. Now I'm curious about your scoring methods."

I pick up a crumb of chicken that fell to the counter and

throw it at him. "What about your ex? Seeking treatment after her time with you?"

A half grin forms on his mouth. "Well, she was delusional, so maybe. It was like two years ago now. Suddenly, she had this idea that we should backpack around the world and both get tattoos. A total 180 from me. No way was that ever going to happen. My office and laptop are my haven, and tattoos on myself are not a thing that I would ever consider. I cut the leash on that one quickly."

"Leash? Huh. That choice of words should be concerning. Then again, you are a career-driven guy and demand everything your way. Maybe a leash is needed."

He answers with his eyes dark and a smirk ghosting on the corner of his mouth. Dangerous too because he's tempting.

"And your desk?"

I glance over my shoulder to my corner. It's my computer with a large screen for editing and a cool keyboard that lights up pink. I like to keep my desk clean and surround it with candles and motivational quotes. I love Post-it notes and pens, too.

"My sanctuary. Don't you have a place like that?" I take a bite of the pizza.

"I tend to work off my coffee table or at the office."

We both chew on our food in silence. Is this awkward? Did I make a mistake asking if he wanted to stay? It just flowed out of my mouth because it seems we are treading toward neutral territory.

"For someone who loves to work, your work atmosphere could improve. Add a little ambiance."

"Maybe sitting on my floor at the coffee table is my ambiance," he challenges.

"You work too much."

His face is brimming with a wry grin. "You've mentioned that many times. Maybe my workload is the way I like it."

"Do you not experience stress?"

He shakes his head. "Long hours only give me more drive. You know what you sign up for when you enter law."

My shoulders bounce. "Okay. An opposite to me. I make my own schedule."

"Good for you. I guess working in a creative field that you only have inspiration when it comes?"

"Yeah, something like that."

Silence shadows us again, and I softly thrum my fingers against the counter. Hmm, what topic can I bring up?

"Your sister!"

Keats's eyes turn peculiar from my sudden outburst. "My sister?"

"Yeah, you mentioned your sister the other night. She visits you a lot."

He swallows and his face turns sullen. "Summer is... my little sister who I love."

"You mentioned she's married?" I wonder.

Keats scratches his chin with the back of his thumb. "Uh, was. Her husband passed away last year."

Instantly, I offer my condolences. "I'm sorry to hear that."

"Well, she is actually now with her husband's brother. It's a long story," he explains.

Bringing my hand to my heart, I feel bad that I asked. But relief hits me when his lips curve up while he is thinking.

"I have a nephew. He's the cutest little guy. I just ordered some toys so I have stuff at my house when he visits. The kid can barely walk but his need to explore runs strong."

Swoon. This man seems to have a connection with kids, and I wasn't expecting that.

Clearing my throat, I try to bury that thought. "That's sweet."

Keats's eyes bug out. "Did you just say sweet in relation to me?"

I point my finger at him. "Don't get cocky on me now."

His tongue swipes to his inner cheek. "I wouldn't dare."

"I only see my family when I want. I'm not much for planning personal stuff. Work, for sure. I mean, I love planning, but the shoots have to be spontaneous in creativity. I'm the same when it comes to seeing family. I like to be spontaneous and don't plan visits until the last minute. No point in pretending that we're all close if we aren't. I guess you wouldn't understand that." Geez, why the hell am I being so open with him?

"I can't relate, but I understand, I guess. You're more a wildflower type. You seem relaxed with life except when it's me."

I throw him a pointed look. "And you seem structured in life except when it comes to me. Suddenly, you're unpredictable."

"Unpredictable… huh." His lips quirk out. "I've never looked at it that way. In work, I can throw in surprises with clauses, but ultimately, the opposing side knows that I will be cutthroat and take no bullshit. And when it comes to other things…" He adjusts his neck. "It can't be unexpected that I'm someone who likes control."

I gently shake my head, amused. "Great self-reflection there. All you have to do is admit that you are a stressful person and I'll give you full credit."

"I'm not stressed," he rebuffs.

I raise my fingers in measurement. "A little stressed… a little cranky too."

He looks unimpressed but then a droll smile appears.

We both nosh on a few bites of pizza in silence, and our eyes catch a few times, which is slightly unnerving because it isn't edged.

"You can't keep reminding me of my life choices. You have work, friends, hobbies. Am I missing anything on that list?"

"Just like you, I'm going through the wheels of motion of daily life. There is nothing wrong with life being content and simple."

Except, I don't have the type of excitement that makes life less boring. Something is missing that I haven't figured out yet. We're supposed to be happy if work is fun, friends are great, and you have hobbies to enjoy. But it feels too easy.

Anyhow. "Truthfully, you're doing me a favor. Leftover pizza in this house turns into breakfast."

Keats smiles gently. "Here I was thinking you wanted my company."

I roll my eyes and think of something funny. "I shouldn't admit this but sometimes I feel like this place is haunted." He doesn't burst out laughing and seems intent on further explanation. "I can't explain it. It's silly, and I don't believe that stuff. But sometimes when I return home, I swear all of the photo frames have been unstraightened or a pillow from the sofa is on the ground."

"Are you sure you don't have a stalker?"

"Nah. I'm too boring for someone to be interested."

"You must go through a lot of salt in this place then. Or do you prefer burning sage? Actually, I bet you haven't yet stocked up on an item made of iron. A horseshoe, perhaps?"

My face squinches. "You're familiar with scaring off spirits?" He doesn't answer, and I sputter a laugh. "Really? No..." It drags out as my face lights up because this is unexpected.

"Didn't see that coming, did you?" he asks, and I shake my head. "In college, some of my roommates were convinced there was a spirit in the place, and we went through everything in the book. Truthfully, after that little phase, the lights no longer flickered at strange moments. Or someone just replaced the lightbulb, I'm not sure. But actually, I would like to think that the presence of someone ghostly was no longer near."

My smile is from ear to ear, as he just threw a wild card at me of the things I never expected him to be interested in. "It could be my great-auntie, but I feel it's a different type of breeze."

"It doesn't have to be a bad thing. When my sister had Christmas at her house, the air was heavy, and I could have sworn it was because her husband who passed was there. How could he not be, you know? Or at least that's what I told her."

Observing him, he is no longer joking. There is a shade of vulnerability, and his facial expression is stoic. To be honest, I'm surprised that he is sharing this with me.

"I can't even imagine how hard it must have been."

He stares at the floor for a second before his eyes strike up and a bit of pep returns. "You should go to Hollows, it's not far from here. There is a candle shop there, and the woman who runs it knows her stuff. She has all of these herbs and oils."

"You're a regular?"

"Nah. But it is a nice little town. Almost thought of moving there until Oliver convinced me otherwise."

"Lucky us," I deadpan. I drop the crust onto the empty lid of the box.

He feigns shock. "You are one of those people who don't eat crust? That's criminal."

"Let me guess. You have the handcuffs," I answer dryly.

The guy winks at me. "You know that answer."

My chest rises as I suck in a big breath. Will we go in circles of flirtation? It's foreign waters for us. Or has everything between us been foreplay all along?

"Did you see old lady Mrs. Tiller watering her flowers the other day in her pajamas?" he asks.

I shake my head. "No, not this time. She told me once that at her age she deserves to live the way she wants and fuck those who judge. She actually loves the F-bomb. I guess she is healthy as a fiddle."

Keats lifts his shoulders up, unsure. "I think she has a daughter who checks in on her."

"The Labrador across the street escaped and stole spareribs that someone was having for their BBQ. Then the kids chased the dog down the street with a squirt gun. Except, Labradors love water, so it was a lost cause. It was cute."

He grins. "We're gossiping about the street together now? You forgot to mention the neighbor who ran their car into my mailbox, except it only seems to have been a nudge. My guess is she was trying to piss me off when she told me."

I click my inner cheek. "Oh, but it was fun."

Keats drops a half-eaten slice of pizza on the box. "Since we seem to be somewhat civil and have gone through our list of questions about each other, do I dare ask…" He seems to be struggling.

My face turns puzzled, and I grab another piece of pizza. "Uhm, not sure what you're thinking." And a lightbulb turns on in my head, causing me to bounce off my stool. "But I can't believe we forgot to open alcohol. I mean, how else will we digest the… recent events." I'm unsure if I phrased that right.

Strolling to the fridge in search of a bottle of wine, I feel eyes on me, even when I open the fridge. Why has Keats gone silent? Is he checking out my ass or something? Holding up a bottle of white, his response is a dangerous laugh under his breath.

"You might want something stronger."

Shrugging, my lips quirk out. "Why? I already made a few bad decisions tonight." It's impossible to hide my smirk.

His brows rise then fall, enjoying my comment. "The thing is, I kind of need a favor."

I stand still with the bottle of white in my hand. "Asking me for a favor is a bold move."

"Really?" He isn't impressed. "I literally carried a box upstairs and then made you come. I think a thank-you might be in order."

Setting the bottle on the counter, something sparks annoyance inside of me. "Seriously? We are doing tit for tat, and now I'm indebted? What in the world could you need from me?"

He circles around the island and approaches me with a cunning appearance and a glint in his eyes. "Agreement, and I have no issue with splaying your legs open again to get that."

Stop it, thighs, do not compress together to handle the sensitive pulse between my legs.

I've never denied that this man is hot as hell, have I?

"Good to know." My tone is flippant as our eyes latch.

"Since we don't involve emotions, you and I, then you're easy—"

I'm quick to protest. "I am not easy."

The corners of his mouth twist as he plants himself in front of me and perches against the counter in a relaxed posed with ankles crossed. "I didn't mean it like that. What I'm trying to say is that I need someone to accompany me for a work function. As much as it pains me to say, you seem to be an option."

"Nope." My lips smack the P. An inkling inside me is leading me in the direction that I think it is. Something to do with said work function.

"Women tend to get a little clingy around me, with unrealistic expectations."

I roll my eyes. "Humble," I say, sarcastic.

He has the audacity to tap his finger on my hand clasping the unopened bottle.

"Come with me." I blink a few times as he observes me. "What a filthy mind you have. To the event, I mean."

Growling, I quickly return the bottle to the fridge, only to immediately walk to the other side of the kitchen to reach up into a cupboard for a bottle of vodka. This conversation is taking a turn.

Opening the bottle, I don't even bother with a glass, and opt for taking a swig. Keats stands there, not having flinched an inch, and patiently watches me, expecting an answer.

"I can reward you with an orgasm or two if you insist. I might even find a leash if you are a good girl."

That stoic confidence laced with humor isn't exactly a turn-off.

Wiggling my finger side to side in the air, I feel my body boiling, and I'm not sure if it's annoyance or... excitement.

"That's not what we are doing." My eyes slide to the side with my jaw joining the ride and return to see that Keats's neutral face remains, not quite believing me.

"When is this thing?" I'll humor us all with investigation.

He smiles brightly. "Next Thursday. Any dress will do."

"Can I still make your life hell?"

Keats stands, satisfied. "Wouldn't expect anything less."

My chin lifts as I study him and internally debate his request. "This is a crazy idea. You know that, right?"

He strides my way with swagger. "It's the safest idea. We both want to throttle one another, therefore, no messy expectations."

"Doesn't this mean I have to pretend to actually tolerate you?"

He hooks his damn finger and slides it along me cheek. That caress, his touch, it sends pulses in all directions within me. "You were not the best actress the other weekend at the murder mystery…" Keats wobbles his head side to side. "But I'm sure you have the performance of a lifetime within you. Hell, we could even role play after if that's your thing."

He comes closer to me with one step. With purpose, he tucks my hair behind my shoulder and brings his mouth to my ear, no touch except his warm breath on my skin, sending ripples through my body. My nipples tighten, and if I'm not careful, I'll be the one to rip his shirt off and climb him like a tree.

"If I do this, then I hope you can keep your hard dick under the radar when in public. I would hate to be embarrassed."

I'm reluctant. I'm reluctant. Keep chanting it. Reluctance means it's a bad idea. Go with instinct, Esme.

His rumble isn't helping, nor is his teeth scraping once against my earlobe. "I have control. You know that," he rasps.

It's barreling up within me. Too fast. "Fine," I say tightly. "I'll do it."

Keats steps away with accomplishment and even swipes my hair back to my front. "So agreeable."

I rub my temples. "I'm already regretting this. You owe me new panties because I've already lost two because of you, and no." I hold my palm up to him. "There will not be any more."

He crosses his arms and now looks serious. "What if there is a sale at the store and you can get three?"

"No." My answer is hard.

"What if I accidentally buy three?" he volleys.

"No," I repeat, and I fold my arms over my cleavage which only perks my breasts up.

"And if your entire underwear drawer goes missing?" He's riling me, and it's working.

I gawk at him. "For someone who went to law school, you are not very smart. Hypothetically if my drawer goes missing then I won't wear anything under my clothes. I'm not sure your little mind and dick could handle that."

His low chuckle reminds me he is the devil. "This is when I would point out in cross examination that you've already experienced my cock, and since you were so full of it, then to call it small is a lie. Further, you get completely drenched for me. Running-down-your-thighs soaking. To go without panties wouldn't be a good idea."

"Your concern is so authentic," I reply in my cynical tone.

Keats claps his hands together once and seems rather chipper. "Three panties it is."

"This is your cue to leave." I don't break my stance.

He makes an effort to move. "You were hospitable tonight, little demon. Thank you."

"Did you do something to the pizza before I came downstairs? Is this some psychedelic experience?"

"Say no to drugs, Esme. Didn't you listen in sixth-grade health class?"

Ruefully I shake my head, realizing I'm seeing a side of Keats where he lets go. The stuffy neighbor that I knew has faded away.

"Get out of here," I say, but my face is relaxed.

He walks to the front door, and I follow. Opening the door, he gives me one last once-over. "Next week then… unless another box arrives and you need to be reprimanded."

"I'm going to throw something at you."

We both have one last stare of… I can't pinpoint what.

But it's different.

And scary.

8
ESME

I push the plate with the blueberry muffin back to Hailey. "No, thanks. I need to fit into a dress tonight."

Foxy Rox is somewhat busy today, so maybe it will drown out the sounds of stupidity in my head.

Hailey drags the plate back in her direction. "More for me." She takes a giant bite while she watches me. "Oh yeah, you have that *thing*." Even when speaking with a full mouth, I can still see the line of a grin.

Shaking my head, I continue to twist the paper wrapper from the straw for my iced tea. "It's just amusement. I would have had a boring evening anyhow." I roll a shoulder back, trying to downplay this all. "Keats can suffer a little bit. I mean, I sure as hell don't plan on being cordial in the car."

She holds up her two fingers. "Twice? Really." I'm regretting that I told her about my recent activities. "What is he…"

My eyes budge out at her. "You want to go down that route? But… yeah, okay, we rip into one another even when doing *that*."

A Cheshire-cat smile forms on her mouth. "This is so awesome. I love seeing people fight attraction."

"Oh, really?" Now I get to smile. "How is that working for ya?"

Her palm flies up at me. "It's different. Oliver is off limits, so that idea can ship on out of my mind."

"Mmhmm."

"Your dress." She's changing the topic. "Classy yet revealing or full on it looks like he is paying for a hooker, and it doesn't look good at a professional function, but you want to piss him off kind of look?"

"I'm not that horrible of a person. I'll keep it classy but not for him. I'm just a beautiful, well-behaved woman who might even find a nice guy tonight."

She sputters a laugh. "You're going to pick up hockey guys?"

A long breath leaves me. "Fine. You're right. I won't. Besides, the text I got just said it's cocktails and that's it."

"Maybe Keats owes you a dinner then."

"Well, I will be starving, so the least he can do is feed me."

I begin to clear my napkin and empty plastic cup. Time tells me that I need to get a move on. Mr. Tight Ass, literally, requests 6pm sharp for departure.

Standing up, Hailey takes my cue as a sign she can now pull out her laptop from her bag to work a little. "I'll let you know if I survive, and if you hear that there is a dead body at the bottom of the river tomorrow, it's completely and utterly not my fault."

Hailey just chuckles as if she doesn't grasp my seriousness.

Which is fair enough because… I hate Keats a little less lately.

"I HATE YOUR CAR." I cross my arms as we continue our drive. I've only been with Keats for five minutes and his cologne and suit jacket with no tie and button-down are already pissing me off.

Keats glances at me then returns his view to the road. "No, you don't."

"Okay, I don't," I give in.

In that moment, I make a point to adjust my dress. It's black because you can't go wrong with black, and it stops just below my knees with heels on. *Except*, when I sit down, the soft fabric can slide up to above my knee if I use my hands just right. Which is exactly what I do.

I don't need to look in Keats's direction to know where his eyes might have wandered.

"Esme, you look… beautiful. Can I say that without you questioning me?"

Be still my heart that turns gray around this man, but he appears genuine.

I've always been told to accept a compliment. "Thank you."

"I don't really see you wear a lot of solid-colored dresses. You are more a jeans or patterned skirt kind of gal."

Lines form on my forehead. "Spying on me now?"

He grins. "Sometimes I see you outside, remember, I'm your neighbor?"

Do not blush. No. No. No.

"It's easier to wear jeans or skirts when taking photos, especially if I have an outside shoot," I explain.

"That makes sense."

"I guess you kind of wear it all. Suits with no tie for work and jeans and tight tees when casual."

Keats throws me a knowing grimace. "Spying on me?" he counters.

Softly, I grumble, "Okay, we've established that we both *might* have noticed what our *neighbor* looks like."

"Anything else we should clear the air about?"

"No. Just tell me how tonight is going to roll."

For a second, Keats focuses on turning at the next light. "It's more an operations and back team event, with the Spinners owner also appearing. So if you were counting on checking out any hockey players then you are in the wrong place, although most of the Spinners are in their mid to late 20s, you little cougar you."

I snort a laugh and not because I'm annoyed, it's just, well, Keats can be funny. It comes naturally to him. On the outside, Keats is the powerful lawyer, always serious and grumpy. However, at random moments he surprises me.

"But seriously, I just want to make an appearance. Probably two drinks tops. Everyone was bringing their other half and it felt like if I didn't then I would be getting a few set-up date requests. Maybe I also want people to see that I have a personal life too. It softens them up and makes them more accommodating when I have a work crisis. Gives the office staff a little extra oomph to hurry things up when I request it."

Looking at him, I grow concerned again. "You had me nearly sympathizing when you mentioned wanting people to see another side of you, but it quickly went downhill when you turned it into a business transaction."

He snickers a sound. "What? It's logistics."

"I can't believe I agreed to this." I slump back into my seat and notice that the woods outside are building up, which means we are getting closer to the vicinity of Lake Spark.

Nature calms me. By no means will I hike all day, but sitting in nature or driving through it is nice.

"Relax. If it helps, I think when eyes land on us, it won't be because of me, it will be you."

One last examination of Keats and he appears somewhat as a normal person again, complete with compliments.

Ten minutes later, we are at the training facility and head inside to a room where they must hold a lot of events. I've been to enough games to know that a hockey game isn't just a game, it's a night full of food, games, and the need to enter raffles.

I'm lucky that the buzzing room doesn't take much notice of us. That's kind of a good thing because then they would notice how Keats's hand is gingerly touching my lower back to guide me toward a waiter walking around with a tray of wine glasses.

Except his need to touch me is a tangled mess of confusion in my head. This is all an act, except somewhere human nature has a desire for it to be possession. My spine straightens at the thought.

Keats takes two glasses of white from the tray and offers me one. "You just assume I like white?" A tinge of attitude is underlying in my voice, but it's purely for banter.

He has a droll smile when he taps his glass to mine. "No. I just remember you pulled out a bottle of white the other day before changing game plans for the vodka."

"Oh." That's true. Apparently, my neighbor is a sucker for little details.

"Keats." A man approaches us from behind and grips Keats's shoulder as a greeting.

"Hey, Declan." Keats smiles then turns to me. "This is Declan Dash, he owns the Spinners." Declan seems to look curiously between us.

"This is my girlfriend, Esme." Keats pulls me closer to his side, his arm looping around my waist, and I remind myself to swallow my disdain that seems to be vanishing.

"Nice to meet you." I shake Declan's offered hand. Keats seems intent to keep his arm in place, and a thump in my chest picks up speed.

It's a friendly introduction, and I guess I will need to get used to this for the next few hours.

"My wife is here somewhere. I'm sure she would love to talk to you."

"That would be lovely."

And sure enough, I'm deposited next to a woman with dark hair and a friendly smile. It only takes a minute before Violet is talking my ear off, and she seems like fun, so I don't mind.

"Trust me, having kids when your husband is so committed to the team makes the moments we get together all the more special. It also means I live off dry shampoo since I'm with the kids the most." She grins to herself then takes a long sip of her drink. "What about you and Keats? Long-term plans?"

I nearly choke on the small cheese pastry appetizer that I picked up from a tray that was floating through the room. "Oh, uh, no. Definitely no kids." A nervous laugh bubbles up. "Besides, he's married to the law," I remark, but really, I have no idea his family plans.

Violet's face becomes doubtful. "Huh. I see him at the Dizzy Duck Inn in town because his sister works there. Totally seems like a kids kind of guy. Or at least with his little nephew he is."

I smile tightly in agreement and decide to change topics. "You must watch a lot of hockey then, I guess?"

Her face lights up. "Of course. I have Declan, and my brother used to play hockey too, then my nephew is captain of the Spinners. It's never-ending. Even the dog has been trained to chase a puck on the ice."

Laughing, it's infectious when people appear out-of-this-world happy. "Sounds like family dinners are hectic yet perfect."

Warm, fun, and new to me too.

That's a vision that frequently pops into my head. I just haven't decided why I don't have an overpowering need to find the right person, nor has it crossed my mind about having kids anytime soon.

We continue our conversation about shopping and day trips to Chicago. The whole time, my eyes occasionally snag a look with Keats who always seems to meet my gaze at the same time. There are soft smiles, a few winks, and a suave hint on his face that is causing a situation between my legs.

When our two hours comes to a close, we even walk back to his car in silence, yet his hand wanders to my lower back to guide me. It's not to tease me, either. The man has manners and can be a gentleman, and I don't think it's to play a part.

It's only when his hand drops away and he circles around the car that we return to normal us.

"Not going to open the door for me?" I chide as he opens his own door.

"Nope. No unrealistic expectations, remember?"

Really? Like really, really? He just drops his manners at the first chance.

We both get in, and now I'm frustrated with him again. "Can we just get back home. I'm getting hangry." I almost pout, and it's all completely true. Tiny pastries only get you so far. His face remains passive as a response.

We drive only a few minutes and then Keats turns the steering wheel so sharply that it causes me to hold onto the door.

"Easy. I would like to be alive tomorrow," I scold him.

"You said you were hangry." Adjusting to my surroundings, I see that we are at a fast-food place with a drive-thru that he's already approaching. "Burger and fries or nuggets?" He sounds easy as a breeze. "A milkshake is probably in order too. Can chill down your body that's probably hot and bothered."

I huff and hold in my grumble. "You are such a piece of work. And no, I don't want a shake," I mock him. "I want one of those apple pie thingies that are really like strudel in a cardboard box."

"Good choice. So, am I ordering for you on the actual dinner part?"

My eyes flutter as I try to take in what is happening. I hate how my need for food outweighs anything on the planet now. "Nuggets with honey mustard sauce. Onion rings instead of fries."

Keats places our order, and he hands me the bag of food while he balances placing the drinks in the cupholders in the middle of the car. Instead of being on our merry way, he drives straight into a parking spot up ahead and turns the engine off.

"If you wanted to stay here, then why not just go inside?"

He begins to open the bag on my lap. "One, because you have this dress on that is far too formal for inside. Two, I'm so fucking hungry that I can't think straight, and it's my cheat day."

It causes me to laugh instantly and relax because he has been holding it in to play it chill. "But now your dear car will smell of food," I tease him.

He turns his body halfway to face me. "I'll take it tomorrow to be serviced and cleaned."

Biting into a nugget, I can't help pointing it out. "That's

such a you thing to say. I know lawyers can make a lot of money, but now you are just showing a little arrogance."

"Except you know that I'm not that bad." Dare I say, there is half a smile on his face.

My hand ducks into the bag to pull out a fry.

"Hey! Stealing my fries? You said onion rings," he jokes.

"What are you going to do? Spank me?" Crap. I responded too quickly without filtering my inner thoughts.

Keats now seems completely entertained. "Such a filthy mind you have. But if you steal my fries then I will have a bite of your pie, the one in the bag, if you needed clarity on that. Since you never bake me one, then this is something close."

Now I wave a nugget at him. "You're nowhere near getting on the list to be a recipient of my baked creations. So, okay, you can steal some of my food if I can get a sip of your shake."

"Your mouth will be where mine has been." He flashes his eyes at me.

A calmness fills the car from our repartee, and we seem to be able to eat in peace.

"Your colleagues or rather the people from the Spinners organization seem nice. Definitely a lot more relaxed than I would expect."

"I can't complain, but I only see most of them at events or when I take a break. Since I'm dealing with confidential information then I'm always behind a closed door or negotiating with sports agents or other teams. You? How long does it take to edit photos or how does it work?"

Leaning down, I sip on his straw without lifting the cup. I peer up to him to taunt him in a playful way, and it only makes him grin. The coolness from the drink is quite refreshing. "No way in hell would I expect you to go for strawberry instead of chocolate."

He adjusts his shoulders and feigns pride on his face. "Gotta keep it healthy and unexpected."

Stifling a laugh, I answer his question. "Normally editing takes a week, but I like to send some first-look photos a day or two after a shoot."

"But never wedding photography? The Dizzy Duck where my sister works seems to have weddings all the time."

"Nah, with wedding festivities it's a long day, or rather the pressure to get the angles and edits right is not my ideal workload. Nobody wants to be on the receiving end of an angry newlywed bride."

"Yet, you like to be on the other end of your neighbor's wrath."

With purpose, I hold up one of his fries. "No comment."

We seem to be staring at one another peculiarly, nearly bashful.

"We need to stop talking about our careers. It's not very compelling, and I think we've established that we both enjoy what we do. Even if one of our jobs might send you into an early heart attack, and it isn't mine."

He doesn't let his smile slip away. "Okay, travel plans? Anywhere you want to go?"

Immediate excitement hits me. "Anywhere it's warm and there is a swing over clear blue water."

"You're a swing kind of girl?"

My face screws. "Actually, I kind of get nauseous on them, but it sounded better in my head. You?"

"Probably also a warm place. Illinois winter is not for the faint of heart."

"You have a heart?"

Keats has a wide grin. "I walked into that, didn't I?"

"Yep."

"Anyhow, a warm place and maybe try scuba diving."

Offering him a nugget, I'm surprised. "I'm trying to decide if you seem like a diver or not."

"Not. The idea of swimming underwater with an oxygen tank seems like hell. But it sounded better in my head."

I'm laughing again. We're two peas in a pod when it comes to conversation and every barb thrown.

"Besides, none of those places have the right liability insurance or verbiage when divers have to sign a waiver of risk."

"You would 100% say that. Consider finding a pastime where you can turn off your career for a hot second."

He grows quiet and scratches his cheek, debating what to say perhaps. "I'm assuming you mean hobbies and not other pastimes."

Right. That's where his mind went.

"Believe it or not, I meant hobbies."

His eyes flick up to meet mine. "Funny that. I don't have time for hobbies because life can give you other pastimes."

Does he mean family? Friends? Sex? I'm confused.

"I think you are more overworked than you think. Or rather you escape by burying yourself in work to avoid something. You just don't know what it is that you are hiding from."

His chin juts out. "You've become a psychologist?"

"No. Just an observer stating the obvious." And I seem to mirror his lifestyle in a way. Am I hiding from something?

"Okay. Well, you are free-spirited because something stable scares the hell out of you."

I scoff a sound. "Let's not go down the road where we analyze one another. We're not drunk enough."

"Hey, you started it."

I admit defeat. "True. So that also means that I can end it."

His lips seal together, and the corner of his mouth lifts. He doesn't press further.

With our food now vanished into our tummies, I quickly exit the car to throw the trash into the container nearby, and of course, Keats revs up his engine while I do that.

Back in the car and our journey home, it's a stiff silence but not the kind we are used to. He is probably in shock as much as I am of how tonight transpired.

"Esme, thank you. I mean it. Dinner with you wasn't so bad, either." His sincerity melts me. Completely and utterly melts me.

From instinct, I reach over to touch his elbow. "You're welcome, and dinner was edible. You should cook more often," I say in jest.

"Maybe so."

My touch drops from him because it's too calming.

What? That simply can't be possible.

"I'm going to have to shower though, I smell like fries," I say.

"Or you just want to shower because my guess is you ruined another pair of panties due to my presence."

Licking my lips, I try to hunker down my smile. "Speaking of which, where are my new panties?"

Keats glances to me, and it feels sinful. "The store only had three-for-one, and someone was adamant that only two will do," he refutes.

"Well then..." My voice is sultry, and it's unexpected. "Looks like I will run out soon and resort to other outfit options—nothing underneath."

His nostrils flare, and his hands tighten on the wheel, with perfect timing as we turn onto our street.

"So, you do want that spanking that I can provide?" There is sexiness to his tone.

"Not sure. I would check now if that's what my body wants but me sliding up my dress would be highly inappropriate for the evening, considering I was promised a gentleman who needed a favor." I'm trying to prod him, my fingers trailing a line from my neck down. I'm a version of myself that was not planned for in his presence.

Parking in his driveway, he turns the engine off with gusto and turns to me with a serious face. "Out of the car."

Ooh, bossy.

Out I go and close the door while Keats walks around the front of his car with his face resigned and eyes narrowing in on me. He stops in front of me and swipes his thumb across his jaw. "Exactly… a gentleman."

That sweltering look that was on my face? It drops.

"Good night, Esme."

And he walks away.

What the hell?

It takes a few seconds of me adjusting to the fact that he is walking into his house without dragging me along.

And why am I so angry that he's doing that?

9
KEATS

Searching the fridge, I don't find what I'm looking for. I completely forgot to pick up strawberries from the store. My sister may be annoyed. Summer gave a list of what to stock since she's staying over with her boyfriend who just proposed, Nash, and my nephew, Bo. Bo can get a little cranky if he doesn't have his snacks; in fact, he stomps his feet and is an adorable little one-year-old. They only live a few towns over but staying over means nobody has to worry about alcohol intake or working around Bo's schedule.

Glancing at my watch, I think I can swing it to the grocery store and back in 30 minutes. Grabbing my phone and keys, I'm halfway down my porch stairs when I see it.

Esme is pissed.

Hair flowing behind her shoulders, arms hanging with fists by her sides, that sexy-as-fuck frown and her near stomp coming my direction. Hurricane Esme, here we come.

"You are the most despicable human on earth."

Before I can even open my mouth, she reaches me and pushes me with her palms against my chest, nearly knocking me back a few steps.

"What the hell have I done now? We are going to have make this quick, I need to run an errand."

Her jaw drops. "Oh, I don't think so, mister."

Esme's brazen demand has my eyes turning to saucers. "Did you wake up on the wrong side of the bed or something?"

"Me?" She points to herself.

"Yeah, you. The one who needs to be tamed."

Her hand lands on her waist and she tips her hip out. "Maybe I would be if you were a normal human being who doesn't just walk away."

Ah. This is about *that.*

"Last night, I was a gentleman."

"Couldn't you just fuck my brains out? I mean, all the signs were there that I would have been on board with that. But *no*, my neighbor from hell decided to head on home."

Proudly I smirk to myself. I mean, I did hold out. That was more because she scares the hell out of me. She thrills me, and last night we kind of just gelled together in conversation. A line between enemies with benefits might have been crossed because, well, we are more than bearable together. For some reason, I thought it was better that we parted ways. I would hate to have crossed the line between pretend date to *hey, this might be an actual date-ish*. Maybe pissing her off a little gave me a rise, too. That makes me the man who should check his sanity, especially since my dick did not appreciate my act of bidding Esme adieu.

Now she's bobbling her head side to side. "You. You dragged me to that party. That's like two social events with you in two weeks. Dragging me along for all of this and ruining my aura," she seethes. "Damn it, murder mystery party."

Gawking at her, I'm now in disbelief that she has some

nerve. "Oh really? I'm pretty positive you got an invite for that too, and it just so happens we ended up driving home together."

She points a finger at me. "You are the worst neighbor. Always such a mind fuck."

Oh, I'm going to challenge her on this. "It's not my fault you voluntarily came home with me and then we—"

"Whoa." That voice is not ours. "We don't need to hear more."

Esme and I zip our attention to my sister who is standing by their car. I didn't hear them arrive.

Nash just smirks because I know he is taking pleasure in this.

I'm frozen, and Esme's mouth is parted open, ready to croak out her death. "How long have you been standing there?" I manage to get out.

"Long enough for me to enjoy this weekend's *roasted* BBQ." Nash has a cheeky smile, because he won't let this go. He turns to open the door to the back to get my nephew from his car seat.

My sister wiggles her fingers to Esme. "You must be the neighbor. I've heard about you. Not exactly in your favor." She smiles tightly. "But you seem to be handling my brother... kind of... maybe."

"Summer," I grit out a warning to my little sister.

"What?" Her voice rises an octave, and she shrugs. "Clearly she returns the sentiment, and it's not my problem that we showed up to your lovers' quarrel."

"We are not lovers," Esme and I say in unison.

Nash just chuckles under his breath. "Sure." He doesn't believe us, clearly.

Well, peachy.

My neighbor just voiced her opinion on my failure to ram

my cock into her last night, and my soon-to-be brother-in-law is ready to have the upper hand all weekend in provoking me.

SUMMER EXAMINES her nails as she sits on the couch in my living room. It's all for show, because in three, two, one… "She seems, uh, nice?"

I rub the back of my neck, feeling a little tense. "A delight." There is zero enthusiasm in my tone.

It causes my sister to chuckle. "Are we on a reverse of roles? Last time, you gave me the romance advice, even though you don't have the greatest track record."

Glaring at her, I don't appreciate my little sister mocking me. "Not a reversal of roles," I firmly state.

She simmers a laugh. "Okay, if that's the case, then it shouldn't bother you if I voice my opinion on your situation. Since, after all, you claim there is nothing going on between you." Summer has a mischievous smile.

"Don't I have a nephew somewhere to play with?" I search the room and stretch to look down the hall.

She swats me. "Nash is getting him down for a nap. Thanks for stocking your house with the portable crib. One less thing to worry about. But don't go off topic. What's the deal with crazy lady who has you completely wrapped around her finger?"

"Or I could have her under my thumb," I counter.

Summer gives me a look that says she's not buying it. "Maybe Esme can join us for the BBQ."

"Absolutely not." That would be a trainwreck of epic proportions since Esme is a loose cannon and Nash can be an ass because it's fun.

"Fine. Are you two like dating?"

My face screws up.

"A benefits kind of thing?"

Quickly, I give her a pointed look. "I am absolutely not discussing this with you for the sake of our sibling relationship."

Summer flaps her hands as if she is a penguin on speed. "Ooh, you are so having a thing with her." She gets comfortable, bringing her feet up and under her while her chin rests on her hand against the back of the sofa. "Is it going somewhere? It seems like she's on par with your need to debate."

I'm going to have a headache by tomorrow. "Simmer it down, oh young one."

She curls her bottom lip, pretending to pout.

"What has Summer in a tiff?" Nash enters the room, as my nephew must have fallen asleep. "Are you not giving her the lowdown on what we witnessed?" He flops down on the chair on the other side of the coffee table, bringing his arms behind his head and throwing his feet up on the table.

Clearing my throat, I give him a warning to get those damn shoes off.

"Relax." He got the hint. "Just remember, the ball is in my court to push your buttons this weekend. I'm going to love every second of this. The neighbor seems to have a thing for you. You two must be having a bad day, though. Don't worry, it will turn around. Fate is fate." There is sincerity in his words because that's how he and my sister happened.

"He's probably not at that stage yet." Summer looks to Nash. "You know, realizing it could be the right thing."

"I can tell. Your brother could loosen up a little. At least he has an excellent wine fridge."

My sister returns her gaze to me. "You can't want to be alone forever. No way. One day you will realize work isn't life." She places her hand on my knee then shakes me. "Let's try to get there before a midlife crisis kicks in."

"What a cheerleader," I rebuke.

"I'm totally in your corner. It just seems like you met your match, and look at that, she's a door knock away. Prime opportunity to keep this thing moving."

I groan and stand up, ready to flee. "You're talking as though I'm seeing Esme. You are like ten steps ahead."

"Uh-oh. Keats said steps ahead. Sounds to me that it has crossed his mind. Time to start shipping Keats and Esme." Nash does a little fist pump in the air and grins.

"Wine. We need wine," I declare.

While they both chuckle, I begin to walk away, only to stop.

"Keats, I forgot to tell you something important," Nash calls out and sounds serious. I turn to answer only to see him holding up a tiny little pearl bead between his fingers. "You really need to be careful. Bo has grabby hands." He is trying not to burst out laughing. "I found this in the hall. Huh, seems to be from a woman's necklace."

Nash and Summer now let loose, and the laughter can probably be heard down the street.

SIPPING MY COFFEE, I feel rested. After BBQing last night and calling it an early night, we all woke a little while ago. I had to check a few emails, but I'm trying to turn off so we can head to the park later.

Nash is busy offering Bo scrambled eggs from his fork as they sit at my kitchen counter. Everything seems quite tranquil.

Tranquil.

Not possible. An alarm goes off in my head, and my head lolls to the side. "Where is my sister?"

"She went for a walk."

Did she?

I quickly stride straight to my front door and open it, only to hear happy voices.

"You're killing me. My brother tried to destroy your box of chocolate?" My sister seems to be best friends with Esme as they stand on the property line chatting.

Casually, I find myself standing next to my sister. "Morning, ladies, what a coincidence that you two crossed paths at eight in the morning… and I didn't know it was chocolate cupcakes. And I didn't try to destroy your box. Not my fault someone thought leaving mail under the front porch bench on an 80-degree day was a smart idea," I grind out because I'm unable to throw on even a pretend smile. Not when I want to grab Esme's arm, haul her inside her house, and kiss her mouth shut.

Esme ignores me and focuses her attention on Summer. "It doesn't matter. I repaid him in full when someone sent him those popcorn gifts and it got delivered to my house, and I made sure that the hole in the box would make the birds happy with a snack." She shoots her eyes at me before whipping them back to Summer. "He is a saint to animals."

Esme gives me a fake smile. "Oh dear, a little grumpy today? It must be a throwback to middle school drama club when you had to perform with a flute in a lion's costume when you were in the Wizard of Oz school play. The cowardly lion suits you."

I zip my sight to my sister. "You told her that?" I nearly shriek.

She shrugs. "What? It's a classic Keats story. Plus, Esme is so fun, I'm sure she appreciates these stories. A photographer, too. I'll need to get your number so I can book a session. "

My eyes bug out between them, and Summer looks at me oddly. "What?"

"I told Esme that I focus on engagement and family photos only, of course." Esme's stare at me is cheeky.

I take a long breath. I don't like being stuck between these two. Not one bit.

"I think I hear Bo crying," I tell my sister.

"Really? I don't hear anything."

"Yeah, screaming," I say dryly.

She waves me off. "Ah, it's fine. Nash is with him." My sister seems invested in continuing the conversation with Esme. "We are probably heading to the park soon if you want to join. I'm sure my brother will say he hates that idea, but he really loves it." If Summer weren't blood related, then I would kill her just for pulling on my cheek like I'm a child.

Esme continues to smile at my sister. "That's sweet of you but I have yoga, and quite frankly, even outside, your brother seems to be tainting the air."

"Really?" I tear my eyes to Esme, and my sharp glare is returned in full. "You want to go down that road this early in the day? Because I could think of about ten ways of how you ruin living on this peaceful road."

She stands taller and squares her body to me. "Peaceful? That's the choice of words that you would like to use? You're being a bit optimistic there."

"Optimism is up your street if you would like to replay the other night."

A hand breaks our wall, and we both snap our attention to my sister who is smiling nervously. "Again. I don't need to hear rehash number two. I already got an earful yesterday."

Esme steps back and smiles at my sister. "It was nice

speaking with you." She takes a few more steps back, and her eyes remain pinned to mine for a few ticks before she turns her back on us.

I watch her leave and hate that I enjoy the view.

My sister interlaces our arms and leads me away. "You are so compatible with her."

Instantly, I look at her strangely. "What planet do you live on?"

She indicates for me to sit on the step with her because a bonding moment is upon us. "Why are you being so stubborn?"

I sigh. "Summer, I haven't been in a relationship in a long time. Why the hell would I even entertain the idea with batshit crazy over there?" Except she's not. Esme is wild, funny, and meets me in the middle of every escapade.

"Liar. You love it. You should ask her out."

I sputter a chuckle. "Why are you pushing this so much?"

"I want to see you happy. I have Nash and Bo, and yes, you are part of my life, but life can be better when you also have your own circle of people close to you. Consider it a bonus."

That does make sense.

"We'll see. I'm kind of busy with the upcoming period. The hockey draft and free-agent player contracts shopping around for teams means a lot of legal documents need to be signed, T's crossed and I's dotted. Not to mention, the sponsors want to relook at terms, oh, and Oliver mentioned about reassessing division of work for next season," I list.

My sister doesn't seem impressed. "Not one thing in that sentence is for you and your personal life. It's really kind of depressing, actually."

I lean back with my arms on a step. "Maybe you have a

point. I'll make a note to buy a plant or something next time I'm at the store."

Summer nudges my arm. "You are annoying and making me kind of angry now. Have you not learned from me that *snap*—" She clicks her fingers. "Everything can change in an instant."

A heavy moment of silence swirls around us. I give her a tight side hug because if anyone can shed some light it's her. She's a widow, after all. "You're right."

"Then open up a little. Tone down the frustration. You two are literally flirting through bickering. The way you look at her and the way she looks at you is so painfully obvious that I'm not sure how your neighbors haven't throttled you two yet. Normally, bystanders are the first to notice."

Smiling to myself, I have to give her props for pushing her agenda on me. The get-her-brother-a-girlfriend agenda.

"Just let us be. Time will tell if we decide to take a step back and be civil. Even if moments have happened that indicate it could be another way, we seem to continue to be only this way."

"Building it up, huh. Just means you are closer to knocking down your wall."

My nose tips up as I observe my sister, oh so wise. "Is it my wall that's the problem? Because I'm not quite sure if it is."

Esme and I are a game of who will falter first. Maybe that's what drives us, turns us on, and if we both admitted it then we would actually have to face one another underneath our exterior. That sure as hell scares me.

"I swear, if next time we visit you don't have a girlfriend on your arm, then I'm going through my contacts to set you up. Except, someone who might be a match for you is a stone's throw away."

"She'll throw the stone back."

Summer's warm smile spreads. "All the more reason she's good for you. My brother always liked a challenge. Please." She brings her hands together in prayer. "Do it for me. If you see a chance to ask her out or make a move or anything that resembles something worth exploring, promise that you will do it."

My sister is convinced that she's right. No chance of even attempting to tell her she's wrong.

Besides, deep down I know everything she says makes sense.

"Promise me. Please, please, please." Puppy eyes. My sister brought out the puppy eyes.

"You sound like the kid I used to take to Jolly Joe's for ice cream. Will you begin to stomp and whine? I need to make you stop because I only signed up for one baby to visit this weekend, not two." I'm playing this off. "Okay."

Summer throws her arms around my neck. "You won't regret it."

"Discussion over. I need breakfast."

She hops up and holds her hand out. "Me too. Breakfast of celebratory champions."

I can only smile back and follow her, letting my eyes wander to Esme's house for a few seconds, wondering what will happen now that my barrier just got thinner.

10

ESME

Walking through the house to the back deck of my neighbor Kelly and Greg's house, I set my envelope with a gift card down on the present table for their son's high school graduation.

A BBQ is a classic way to celebrate this momentous occasion. They have family and friends here, but also neighbors… including Keats. With what now feels like second nature, my eyes drift to him as soon as my peripheral view spots the man of my contempt.

He has a beer bottle in one hand, quickly sliding his phone into his pocket with his other, all while chatting to Oliver. Maybe it's his wolflike senses, but he must feel my eyes on him as he shoots in my direction. There is no point for me to look away, as it is obvious that we are already trapped.

Internally, I'm cursing early summer because I'm wearing a casual dress which means the only layer between him and my pussy are thin panties. I can't afford for my body to find Keats attractive or to remember the way he kisses with reverence and command. But I also remember the other day where

I was a little heated with anger in his yard, with his sister breaking the scene. I'm a little bit mortified from it all.

I'm nearly startled by a hand touching my elbow from the side. "Thank you so much for coming," Kelly greets me.

My eyes zip away from Keats, and I offer her a smile. "Of course, you must be excited for Ryan and the big milestone."

"We are. College flips my mind upside down. He's grown so fast, and it will be hard having him around less, but luckily, we still have a ten-year-old to keep us busy."

"Not a dull moment then."

Kelly glances away then her eyes draw a line back to me. "I guess you two must have a truce or something since neither one of you have ripped the other to shreds yet."

I smirk to myself. "Yet." My brows rise from the reality of how I communicate with Keats.

We are so ridiculously immature and even we know it.

"Anyhow, I should make my rounds. Ooh, did you see Mrs. Tiller knitted Ryan a hat for winter? He'll never wear it, but it's still adorable."

I chuckle. "I can guess that wouldn't be a major fashion choice, and of course, make your rounds. Thanks for inviting me."

My smile drops when I realize the inevitable looms. I can't erase the other day in my state of crazy, nor can I avoid Keats in a backyard. Inhaling all of the air I can, I gear myself up and tread in Keats's direction.

Immediately, Oliver gives me a polite smile before his eyes swing to study his friend. The man whose eyes are fixed on me and making me feel anxious.

Oliver is the first to speak up. "Good to see you. You know what, I think I'm going to grab a burger now and catch up with my brother." Oliver tips his bottle up to me, and the man is smart to disperse into the party.

"Isn't it funny how we all call him Sheriff Carter even when he's off duty, but everyone just seems to roll with it." I'm puzzled.

Keats doesn't reply, but we are alone now. No way am I going to grovel, but I'm not going to cause a scene. I don't wish to fight with him.

"Hi," I begin softy with a weak smile.

"Hey."

"Seems like we both had the same idea... to drop off a gift and steal some food." Small talk is a start, right?

His lips roll in, and his entire body seems to be in neutral mode. "Or we both had an invite and it's the polite thing to do to make an appearance... and yes, nabbing some food is also a bonus."

The brief pause appears to mean that we are both on the same level of awkwardness. But I take the plunge.

"I'm sorry." It bursts out of my mouth. His eyes haven't moved, which is why my gaze sinks down to the wood paneling of the deck to avoid his eyes, and he patiently waits for me to say more. "I'm sorry, okay? There I said it."

"Care to elaborate?"

Damn it, he's really going to draw this out for his personal enjoyment. "Storming over to your lawn as if I was a woman possessed, only for your sister to show up and hear it. Impeccable timing, huh?" My eyes swim to the side, and maybe there is a smidgen of humor in this whole situation.

Keats's mouth is stretching into a smirk. "An apology. I can't believe you actually just showed your un-demon-like qualities," he teases me, and that causes a wave of relief to wash over me, and my face relaxes. "And I kind of... well, also didn't seem to help."

I blink and bite the corner of my mouth. "Can we also forget about what I said?"

His chuckle causes me to sense a little cockiness boiling up within him. "Not a fucking chance. My neighbor stormed over because I didn't fuck her brains out, which means that she very much enjoys my cock."

Instantly, I panic and search for any bystanders that may be around. "Say that louder, will ya?"

"I could." He grins.

I sigh, pushing away any sliver of his banter that I sometimes relish and decide to stick to being practical. "Just let's forget about it. Everything from the past few weeks. We can pretend that it never happened and focus on our mail mishaps."

I just laid out a horrible idea. Nothing about that is appealing, which means I need to check my sanity. Except, no attachments, right? That's what he said once, and I think it's what I want too, so I guess my words make sense.

"Grand idea then," he answers tightly. It takes me aback for a second. I kind of assumed he would be a bit more chipper on the fact that I'm following his policy. Instead, his eyes lower and his face drops for a second.

But I move us along as I brush my hair all to one side over the front of my shoulder. "Uh, how was the weekend with your sister?"

"Yeah, good as always. Did the whole park thing, baby swings, then hit up Foxy Rox for a coffee, and apparently babyccinos are a thing."

I laugh, but it's mostly to cover up the fact that I feel flustered from the imagery in my head. "Yeah, I've heard something about those. Foxy Rox has a whole menu for kids' and puppies' drinking and snacking needs. I mean, not that a human child is the same as a puppy or a puppy is the same as a human. It's more like treats made out of oats and low sugar. For the dog, of course. Treats are for dogs and snacks are for kids. And pupcups are just pure whipped cream, I think, which pretty much defeats the whole low-sugar thing." I'm rambling a mile a minute.

Watching me this way doesn't seem to deter his smile. "Thank you for the explanation of biology and menu items."

My face turns crimson because I'm aware that I'm twisting my words, all because Keats causes knots inside of me, but I hate to admit that. "Uhm, I just wanted to apologize since you are here, and now I have, which means I can conquer a snack plate of veggies and dip with a few cookies on the side."

I don't even let him answer me because I scurry away, leaving him to watch me and the sway that I consciously do. Is he as lost in his thoughts as I am in my own? I'm trying to digest the shift in the air because I'm not sure what just happened. We're in neutral territory, right? Our hostile moments are over, no? He's pulling me in, and that simply can't be possible.

The thing about late-afternoon BBQ graduation parties is that the teenagers tend to leave after dinner to check out the next party on their schedule of friends heading to their next life chapter. It also means that the adults stay behind and continue to drink. Moving on from beer and wine, the parents, or rather, the mother of the graduate, is now mixing margaritas and letting a little loose.

A few of us keep going on this train. Kelly and Greg are cool. I'm confident Greg will break out his guitar at some point and jam to a classic alternative song.

With the hanging lights on and a buzz flowing through

me, I'm going to agree that Kelly is excellent at whipping up an alcoholic beverage.

"I should head out. I know Kelly and Greg had their son young, but it kind of unnerves me to see two parents around our age with a teenager. Suddenly, I feel old," Oliver remarks as he downs his last sip of, well, I'm not sure what.

We're sitting in a row on the bench, with Keats on his other side.

I glance down to my cup and see that I'm running dry, too. "It's kind of fun. Let them be in their element. I don't often see them get a chance to let loose."

"Because they're domesticated," Keats notes with distaste.

"Ugh, now I remember why I don't like you. What a judgmental ass."

Keats pops his head out to peer around Oliver. "Really? You want to go down this route? We were doing so well."

Oliver groans, aggravated. "You two are like children who need a timeout."

"Sorry if Mr. Uptight needs to be called out. I bet he even tattles on Ryan when he throws parties when his parents are out of town." Keats doesn't answer but adjusts his neck as he stiffens. "Are you kidding me? You do, don't you? You need to loosen up."

Oliver's eyes turn to saucers, and he stands at the same time. "That's my cue to head on home."

Keats and I join him on the departure. "Don't even tell me to relax or I swear to God there will be consequences." The grit in his tone makes it clear the true meaning of his dirty words.

"That's it. I'm saying goodbye and leaving you two to work out your aggression issues, because I sure as hell don't want to be a witness."

Keats and I follow Oliver but not without throwing one another glares. We all bid farewell to the hosts after repeating our congratulations and make our way to the street. Oliver waves us off before he walks down the street to his house. He's in no mood for further conversation.

"You are so intolerable. What was that? Consequences. Ooh." I wiggle my fingers in the air. "Let's just let anyone in earshot hear you confirm that you have control issues when your dick wants to play."

Now I'm 100% confident that frozen margarita was a little strong.

"What a vulgar little demon you are." He crosses his arms.

I grumble in exhaustion. "We are so fucking immature around one another," I point out.

"Oh, I agree. Our game of cat and mouse is anything but mature. But it makes me feel rejuvenated and less uptight, as you call it."

My brows raise in astonishment at his admission. I roll my shoulder back and lose my words because we seem unusually aligned. "Well…good. I guess we are on the same page there."

The air grows silent as we both realize that fact.

Under the streetlight we seem to be having another one our traditional conversations. Only when my head tilts to the side do I realize that neither one of us have moved as we stand by our mailboxes. The center of our universe.

It doesn't take long for Keats to recognize our setting, and for an inexplicable reason, our flared tempers seem to flatten and disappear. Instead, we stand in silence. He crosses his arms over his chest, and I nibble my bottom lip. Neither one of us is moving our feet. We're near unwavering.

What were we even talking about? It isn't helped by the

fact that we are both staring at two mailboxes to ensure our eyes don't meet.

"Want to open a bottle of bad bourbon?" I ask in a monotone because the past few minutes of bickering are now history.

"Yes," he replies bluntly. "Should we fuck this out?"

"Yes."

"Do I get to yank your hair and spank you if needed?" He's very serious.

"Obviously, yes." I'm serious too as we don't stare at one another.

"Any special requests?"

I turn my head to him. "Why yes. Stop cross-examining me, and let's get inside."

He's satisfied with my words.

We don't say anything as we totter to my house and up the steps. The man even leans against the door as I unlock it, clearly confident enough to be comfortable.

When inside, I don't even bother to look at him as I nearly dart to the kitchen, open my cupboard, and pull out a bottle of bourbon. It's only when I look around my kitchen island that I finally have the vision of Keats, again in my home.

He's relaxed on the couch, with his feet on the coffee table as he leans back with his arms behind his head. If I wasn't on a mission to get tipsier, I would laugh. The man is all suits during the day, but he unwinds when it involves a woman with a potential for no talk.

Reaching the couch, I knock his legs off with my knee and plant my feet down in front of Keats, with my eyes alluring as I unscrew the cap of the bottle.

"No glasses?" His eyes stake me with a hint of playfulness as the corner of his mouth tugs.

"Nope," I respond sharply and then take a swig of bourbon.

Offering it to him, he grimaces and eagerly takes the bottle, ensuring his eyes pin mine. One swallow and I give up on trying to hold up the pretense of having a drink.

Slowly, I crawl on top of him and only stop when my thighs are firmly squared to his waist as I straddle him and lift my body slightly. A sly smirk lifts my lips, and with purpose, I snatch the bottle back and drink a sip, well aware that my mouth around the bottle is making him crazy.

"We don't need glasses," I clarify in a raspy voice. "And no, don't add that to the list of why you need to show me *consequences,*" I mock.

That match inside of me strikes with an overriding need to take control of our dynamic. I'm taking the wheel tonight. As I bring the bottle to his lips, he drinks what I offer with our sight remaining chained to one another.

"Open again," I request, and when he listens, I lift the bottle higher to pour from above into his mouth, quickly slamming my lips down onto his to taste the alcohol, sucking the liquid from his mouth to drink. Because Keats is on the same wavelength as me, he doesn't hesitate, and his fingers fist the hair on the back of my head to yank me back slightly.

With his free hand, he grabs the bottle and pulls my head back enough for him to pour a few drops onto the slope of my neck, instantly trickling down my skin. Keats's tongue darts out to lick my body, and it takes all my power to keep my pussy clenched, as he just sent a rocket to my clit.

"Of course you like to get wet around me." His face turns menacing right before he paints my lips with the rim of the bottle, leaving a trail of alcohol.

He crashes his mouth down on mine, and I'm thankful

that the thoughts of grabbing glasses never once filled my mind.

My hips roll in a wave on top of his shaft that is straining to break free from under his jeans.

Clasping the bottom of my dress, I swiftly peel it up until I'm left in my bra and panties. I work fast, tugging and pulling his shirt until it's off.

We still for a second, and I realize that Keats is surveying me, enamored, and stars burst inside me from the way he sears me with his eyes.

"You wear lace and liquor well." His hands drop to splay against the bottom of my spine as he tips me back gently, his lips sweeping up where the drops of liquid stop, and it leads him straight to the edge of my bra cups.

His fervent need and his five o'clock shadow rubbing against my skin bring out a small breathy yelp from me as my entire body tingles. Keats licks until he switches to his teeth, grazing my cleavage and placing delicate kisses.

I'm desperate for more. I straighten my body and sit up for more stability. His eyes gleam with curiosity as I take control of the situation. Slithering down his naked chest, I blindly search for the bottle that at some point was placed on the floor. Once found, I bring it just high enough above him and drizzle a few drops over his chest.

I lower my mouth to his pecs and murmur against his skin. "We don't like one another," I clarify then kiss his chest.

He shakes his head in disagreement but continues to let me kiss down the core of his body. "But we seem to agree on one thing, Esme."

I throw him a sensual look as I walk back on my knees to unbuckle his belt. "Oh yeah, and what is that?" I ask.

Keats has that melting look again. "That my cock feels good inside you."

I can't help but bubble a laugh under my breath. "Fine. We have an agreement, hooray us."

His hands snap to grip my upper arms so tight that I'm not sure if it hurts or not. "On top of me, *now*."

"And if I don't?" I challenge, my head cocking to the side.

He's already hauling my body back up until I have no choice but to sink down on top of his lap.

"So help me, I'll spank you until your ass is red tomorrow."

Fire. My body is on fire.

God, this man speaks to my dirty soul.

"By all means, do," I counter.

I'm not sure who makes the move, him or me, but our mouths create tremors and soon our bodies are twisting around one another. Keats, the man who always has his own way, throws me onto my sofa with my back against the cushions.

I'm going to scream if he doesn't slam into me in the next few seconds. I'm craving him.

It scares me that we seem to be able to read one another's minds, because he fulfills my wish, and I shamelessly let a loud moan leave my lips.

Between the alcohol and his talented body, my head spinning and his touch leaving me extra sensitive, I dig my nails into his back to hang on because I'm on a ride that feels like flying. The temperature of my body feels like a fever, but it makes this all the better.

This experience only heightens when even in my tipsy state, I acknowledge that this has nothing to do with my drink choices tonight. This feeling is all Keats. I'll assess that later, because right now I'm surrendering to him, giving him my body because he identifies every little spot I have to ensure I see fireworks.

And not wanting him to stop is beginning to feel like more than just tonight.

My sofa might be ruined, but I don't care. Not after that orgasm I just had. We are squished together, both lying on the couch, completely wrecked and spent.

"I need a cigarette," I comment as I stare at the ceiling, noticing my bra-covered chest lifting and dropping from my breathing.

"You used to smoke?" Keats sounds surprised.

I smile to myself. "No. But it sounds good after the way you fuck." It's an out-of-body experience, to be honest.

He chuckles, and my treacherous body decides that my head should rest against his chest. It must be an invitation for his arm to curl around me because that's what he does. The air-conditioning in the room chases the warmth away from my body as a chill hits me, and Keats reaches to grab the throw blanket hanging on the back of the sofa to drape across our bodies.

"Don't you dare bring that blanket over us," I warn.

"Now I'll do it just to piss you off," he jokes.

The blanket feels smooth against my body, even though he only covers us to the waist. I guess this is okay. It's not full-on nuzzling together. I can handle this. No dangerous territories entered.

Still, I feel the need to point out, "We don't do cuddling, we bite." My serious tone only receives a deep chuff as a response.

"Give me your finger, Esme," he orders. Holding one up,

he's quick to capture it between his teeth with a light bite before he drags his lips off, sucking gently. "There."

My body is trying to weigh down on this couch because his action just turned me on again.

"I guess that will do."

Keats drums his fingertips on the curve of my shoulder, and we seem to be stewing in the moments after sex. "What's that over there?" His bumps his nose up.

I search for what he could be looking at, and I burst out with a laugh. "You mean the bumper sticker?" It's propped up by a basket of books sitting near my TV; I saw it the other day at the gas station.

"It says 'I stop for anything with legs,'" he reads.

I use the nail on my index finger to draw a circle on his chest and cluck my tongue. "I have that in case you piss me off too much, and I'll just put it on your car when you're sleeping."

He doesn't seem to be amused as I can feel his body tense slightly, but then it eases just as fast.

Quiet happens again, and we just lie here, near comatose.

I refuse to concede that our bodies mold when in this position next to one another or how comfortable I feel in his arms.

"I'm curious if Kelly will be hungover tomorrow," I wonder.

Keats squeezes my arm. "I'm curious if *we* will be hungover tomorrow."

I swat his chest. "Nah, you fucked me sober."

He laughs at me, happily content with my humor.

"Anyhow, she deserves it," I add.

Keats mumbles a noise in response before he blows out a long breath. "Why am I lying here and not leaving?" he thinks aloud, his fingers skimming down my arm, and he doesn't even seem to recognize the affectionate move.

"Recovery time," I supply.

"Before we would have escaped as fast as can be. I guess something always eventually happens to change perception, and it's safe enough not to kill one another for our indiscretions."

As much as he is trying to joke, I can't help sense that an uncharted territory is looming in the distance. I think I might hope so. Lately, every moment around this guy feels like another pebble gone on the long path to a destination that I'm not quite sure of.

"No need to process it now," I suggest. It's the safest option.

He pats my arm to inform me that the moment is over. We begin to squirm until we are both off the couch and redressing with whatever fell to the floor. It's funny, this is as naked as we've been, and I'm still wearing a bra.

"The fact is we crossed into enemies-with-benefits territory," he highlights.

"Don't make me think right now," I beg drowsily.

"Everyone is searching for someone, even if they don't realize it," he mentions.

My face puzzles. "I'm not that someone."

Keats stretches his shirt over his head. "I just meant you're the kind of woman who is waiting for a husband."

I scoff at the audacity. "Where is this coming from?"

He shrugs. "I'm just saying that if you think you want to find Mr. Right, then let me know and I will be sure to go back to annoying you ten out of ten on the scale, in place of our current sixish."

Fluttering my eyes, an unexplainable anger begins to brew. "What about you? Surely, someone will cross your path, dying to be married to a lawyer who ignores her half the time due to work."

"I don't want that."

Shaking my head, I need to point out his own logic. "You said it yourself, 'everyone is searching'... and last I checked, you fall into the everyone category."

The corner of his mouth hitches up. "This discussion is heading too deep."

What in the world? How do I go from vaguely noticing that this guy is igniting new feelings in me to unbelievable exasperation? "Then don't say something like that."

Keats shakes his head. "Relax. I'm just letting you know the options. Do I need to bury my cock into you again so you can calm down?"

Tempting.

"Well, this has been fun." I drag my words out flatly. This is the safer bet.

He stifles a laugh. "Hint taken."

But as he leaves, I'm trying to bury the feeling that there is a morsel of disappointment that he mentioned searching. I'm beginning to fear that I should explore if there is any possibility he may be that someone.

11

KEATS

Arriving home, I carry my small grocery bag of chicken, broccoli, and garlic when I arrive home. The can of nuts are for snacking; they're my downfall because they are salted and not good for my slim physique. Halfway up my porch stairs, I remember.

Mail. I need to check it.

Setting the bag down on a step, I saunter down my driveway. A giggle fills my ears. I look across the street to see our neighbor's contractor talking with Esme. Pretty seems like a word for a teenager with a crush, but right now, that's the word that comes to mind when I look at her. I'm enjoying the warm weather; it means her legs are often bare. What I don't appreciate is that she's batting her lashes, and her smile must hurt.

"Come on, one drink." The contractor, Dave, I think is his name, holds up one finger and seems to be pleading.

Esme smiles. "Really, I think my weekend is full."

"Then what about Tuesday?"

"Tuesday would imply dinner as well."

Holy shit. Are they flirting with one another?

"I can do that," Dave responds.

Esme laughs. "Good to know, but Tuesday looks to be a long day of shoots, so it's not a great idea."

All her answers are the correct ones that make me internally repeat good girl, but I still don't like this situation one bit.

While I pretend to check my mailbox, they don't seem to notice that they have a spectator. I half turn and probably have a cold look on my face, with my eyes darkened. I'm irritated by witnessing this and more possessive than I could have imagined when it comes to Esme.

"Thursday? My heart's going to break if you say no. I see you every day and have been waiting for the right time to ask."

"I think Thursday she's busy," I pipe up.

Their heads swing in my direction to look at me from across the street.

"Keats?" Esme appears to be completely surprised and puzzled.

Closing my mailbox door with a forceful push, I take a few steps toward them. "Sorry to interrupt this little conversation. Neighborhood watch has a thing about checking in with neighbors who find themselves in conversations with strangers."

The dude looks at me, dumbfounded. "Uh, you've seen me here for a few weeks while I work on the Millers' kitchen."

Esme seems to be fuming and lets me know by slicing me with a pointed look that only I can see. "Thank you for your concern but all is okay. Have a lovely night." Ooh, there's venom under her tone, but only I would know that. Davey here is oblivious to how I bring out this side of Esme.

"No can do." I hold up the three letters I received, of

which two are probably junk mail. "We have another mix-up," I lie.

Her loud sigh can probably be heard down the street. "Look at that timing... so convenient." Her contrite smile slays me every time. She looks back to Dave. "Sorry. I need to get something in the oven *for dinner* and have to handle this mail situation. Maybe we will chat tomorrow, a coffee perhaps."

Dave's eyes zoom between Esme and me. "Yeah... sure." If he feels as though this situation just took a turn and that he shouldn't involve himself in our mess, then he gets a gold star for correctly analyzing this.

"Keats," Esme grits out as she grabs my arm and marches us to my door. She huffs, nails clawing into my arm, and my astute grin stretches on my face. We move fast in our stomp with my small bag of groceries falling off the step in our war path.

She abruptly stops at the bottom of the porch stairs and lets go of my arm. "I'm returning you to your cage and saying adios. So just give me the letter." She holds her palm out.

"Follow me for a second." I step up, and she surprisingly follows. Opening my door, we arrive inside, and I close the door behind me.

"Letter," she bites out, motioning with her hand to give it to her.

"No can do. There isn't actually any mail for you." Honesty always wins, and in this case, I earn her growl which causes my dick to twitch every single time.

Her mouth opens but no voice can be heard because I'm slamming my lips down onto hers, guiding her back to my front door. In one thump, I have her trapped. Parting our mouths, I raise her arms above her head, shackling her wrists, and spear her with my determined gaze.

"Here is the thing. I don't fucking share."

Esme's entire face blazes with excitement, and I see that she's staring at my mouth.

"I'm not yours," she whispers in her gravelly voice, issuing a challenge.

I'm quick to anchor my hand down between us, to touch her panties with her skirt now bunched at her waist, and she gasps. "I beg to differ. As long as you and I keep playing this game and my cock ends up in this pussy, then I'm not sharing. You're mine."

Our lips meet again for a rough and urgent kiss with her body pressing against mine.

Pulling the fabric to the side, I explore her already drenched pussy, my fingers going straight to her clit.

Esme coos a moan.

"Like that?" I husk.

She nods, her eyelids hooding closed.

No foreplay. Not now.

It's a blur how I drop to my knees, drag her panties off, place a few kisses up her legs then stand before her as I unbuckle my belt.

I flip her around with her palms smacking against the door. The moment I slide into her, our sounds merge as one. I press further inside of her, and I can feel her body quiver. I encircle her wrists to keep them firm against the door above her head as I deliver a blunt thrust.

"Don't stop," she breathes with her cheek flat against the surface.

"I won't if you tell me you understand. This pussy is mine."

She bites into my arm. It's not because she's angry, it's because my thrusts are hard and unforgiving. I wouldn't be this way if I didn't think she wanted it, but I've already learned that our sexual wants are aligned.

"It's yours. I only belong to you," she rasps, and she purposely draws me closer by pressing against me.

"That's settled then. Now let me ensure that you won't be able to stand tomorrow."

We work together so well that I'm not sure who is slamming into whom. Our bodies are flush, bringing us together as one, and my door is getting pounded and our breaths fast and heavy.

She turns her head to glance over her shoulder for a crushing kiss. It's unforgiving, and we only give more, our tongues joining in on the ride by twirling around the other.

Holding her tight, we both work our way together to our end. Unloading into her, I'm seeing stars when I come with her. Only with her. Esme strokes her clit until she shakes around my cock, causing me to slip out.

I don't like it when she slides away, but gravity is gravity.

She trudges up straight, and I step back, worn out yet still able to close my pants.

Our panting begins to subside, but Esme turns, with her back against the door for support, as she doesn't seem to be able to move. She's in a daze, with her hair wild and lips swollen. A beautiful mess that's all my doing.

I return to her, swooping down to snatch up her panties. Our eyes lock as I step closer to her with the distance only just enough to enable me to tuck between us to wipe between her legs. The act alone is sensual and slow as our eyes don't drift. Her breath speeds up as I clean her. I fix her skirt that is no longer gathered up, and I throw her balled-up panties to the side.

But now we need space, and the silence is electrifying yet unclear.

"We keep finding ourselves in this situation," I note softly.

Esme smooths her hair. "I've noticed."

My head bows low, the back of my finger tracing a line along my chin. What in the world do we do now?

And she answers.

Esme points her finger at me with emotion flaring up, and now I'm certain that this is her defense mechanism. "How dare you think that at the snap of your fingers you can just order me around because you have some greedy thought. Let alone that I will just fall at your feet."

I shouldn't smirk because if she's upset about this then she has a right, and I should respect that, except I can clearly see that it's not the case, which is why I can prod her a little. "But you did. You agreed to be only mine, remember?"

Her facial expression strains, and she's doing her best not to throttle me. She pivots to open my front door but pauses. "You are—"

"The guy you were angry at because I didn't fuck you then."

Esme tries to inhale a calming breath. "Well… maybe I figured out that I deserve more and shouldn't get caught in these… moments with you." She turns without closing the door, and I follow and stop to lean against the doorframe to watch the back of Esme who seems in doubt about where she is going as she wrestles with herself at the bottom of my porch stairs.

"I mean, we haven't even figured out if this is a benefits kind of thing or like, I don't know." She's speaking to herself and has no idea that I'm listening. "But no, I'm in a situation where lust makes me do stupid yet delicious things that gives me an O or two. Esme, no. A gentleman, that's what I want… or maybe I want a date."

"Then go on a date with me," I say unceremoniously. It isn't even me throwing something out there without thought, it's just what it seems to be—my thoughts finally agreeing with my actions.

My voice startles her, and she slowly turns on her heels to face me, now aware that I've been listening. I don't flinch and remain in my spot with ankles and arms crossed and my shoulder against the door. "Go on a date with me," I repeat because her eyes seem wary.

Her mouth opens but only small snippets of a croaked sound escape.

"Well? I don't have all day to wait for an answer." I pretend to be inconvenienced.

"A date?" Her eyes change brightness as she asks.

I scratch my cheek as I pretend to ponder. "Yeah... I believe I said that."

I can't read her, but then her demeanor changes to near sweet. "A date with me?"

Puffing my cheeks out, I thought we would get here sooner. "Yes, you. To clarify, you on a date, with me, but I need an answer—"

"Yes." She doesn't give me a chance to finish.

We stare at each other, aware that we've taken another twist that seems we both wanted.

12
ESME

Giving myself the once-over again, I pucker my lips to get another layer of lip balm on. As much as I'm going to tease Keats for not picking me up at my door, I think it would be a little too classic and make the uneasiness of how we are approaching this date a little odder. Plus, he is coming home from work, and I will jump into his car at the curb. A sort of drive-thru but picking up a date instead.

I'm dressed in a casual cotton dress that maybe clings to my body, with sandals. I threw on hoop earrings and several bracelets. With no clue what we will be doing tonight, I'm still eager, and I open the door and quickly lock it behind me.

"Oh hello, dear." Immediately I hear Mrs. Tiller call out.

Looking to the house next door, I see that she is watering her potted plants. "Keeping busy, I see. I guess we haven't had a lot of rain recently." Smiling, I make my way over to the property line for a little chitchat while I wait.

"You look all dolled up. A date?"

My smile stretches more, but I look away with the hope

that she doesn't see me looking so timid. "Something like that."

She turns her hose off. "With our dear neighbor?"

My face squinches. "Yeah. How did you know?"

"Kelly across the street said her contractor mentioned that someone got a little territorial with the neighbor he was trying to ask out. Naturally, Kelly asked me if something was blossoming between our two neighbors, and we both hope it will take the street arguments down a notch. Then, of course, young Oliver who lives down the street and works with your new beau was more than eager to give his two cents when he was out for his run. Then we have the Browns' kids who mentioned they saw Keats collect your pizza box at your door the other week. Neighborhood watch also started a separate email chain to discuss our theories."

My entire face drops from the happenings going on around my back. "Wow, that's… I have no words," I reply blankly.

She assesses me. "Are you sure you don't want to grab a light sweater?"

"No. I'm fine."

She cocks her head to the side gently. "Just a little coverup or something. You don't want to give your gentleman caller the impression that you are too easy."

"What the hell," I mumble to myself. What is happening? Nervously, I do my best to keep my face bright. "Really. I'm not chilly." Besides, Keats had already done indecent things to me.

I never knew that I would be so thankful to hear Keats's car drive up the street.

"Oh, look at that. I need to run. Don't forget your tomato plants in the side yard."

"You two kids have fun. Don't be out too late."

I almost skip to the street, and Keats doesn't even have opportunity to fully stop because I already open the passenger's side door, and for the brief few seconds he does stop, I slide onto the seat in record time and close the door.

"Go. Now. Hurry."

Keats looks at me strangely but listens, with his foot on the accelerator. "What in the world?"

Buckling up, I take a deep calming breath. "Mrs. Tiller was giving me fashion advice, as I'm apparently encouraging you to be an improper gentleman caller."

He snorts a laugh. "She's not exactly wrong."

I glare at him that I'm not amused. Not because it isn't funny. "There's more. The entire street has been talking about us. Even secret conversations and bets, I'm sure. If you actually show me your A-game tonight, then neither one of us can enter the other's house because someone from neighborhood watch will be out with their binoculars and inform everyone by 8am tomorrow."

Keats just chuckles. "This is classic. Another reason I live on Everhope Road. We have a great cast of characters."

My smile is uncontrollable at this point. "You're not the one that Mrs. Tiller is probably now knitting a sweater for, as I'm apparently dressing too scandalously."

Keats grows quiet for a second, calming down. "You look good," he comments in earnest.

Taking in my surroundings, I remind myself why I'm here.

On a date.

With Keats.

For a man who probably just worked a 12-hour day, he seems refreshed. My favorite, with a few buttons undone, and his cologne with a tint of nutmeg tingles just right to my nose.

"Thanks. How was work?"

"The usual. Those are for you, by the way." He motions with his head as his eyes remain on the road.

It doesn't take long for me to search the back, as the bunch of flowers are on the middle of the seat. Maybe he noticed my wildflowers in a vase near my desk when we shared pizza and that's why he chose this bouquet. It's a far-too-sweet gesture, even for me, but oh gosh, I like it.

"They're lovely."

Right away, he seems proud of himself. "I was debating on a fruit basket, but that would insinuate you would need to make me a pie, and that's more serious than marriage, so we are not going down that road."

I laugh softly. "For a man who is a little high-strung, I never expected you to be… funny? Relaxed? Somewhat normal." My face must show that I'm unsure how to phrase that.

He glances to his side with feigned shock. "Thank you, I think."

Another thought dawns on me. "Where are we going, by the way? You never mentioned. This is your make-it-or-break-it moment on the dating front."

"You're going to be surprised again."

"Oh yeah?"

"How do you feel about bread-making and wine?"

Lines form on my head. "As in…"

He laughs to himself. "The Riverbell by the dock, they have a wine-and-loafs night once a month, and it just so happens that tonight is the night." The moored riverboat is a restaurant that is borderline casual.

My brows rise, as I'm very impressed. "So, like a wine tasting with cheese and bread?"

"Sourdough bread. Not just any bread. Let's get that clear. It's a classy bread."

Sputtering a laugh, I love this. "This is a first. Inventive, for sure."

"I passed the make-it-or-break-it test?"

"With flying colors."

Since we only need to park by the river, the drive is quick and parking is a breeze. He even opens my door, and I'm not sure if it's to be genuine or to tease me about last time.

Either way, I'm already having fun, and when we walk up the dock onto the boat, there's a nice vibe inside. The restaurant was refurbished a while ago, and inside are hanging lights, and the industrial feel gives an alternative flare. I see a long table, and we take our seats next to one another.

The cheese plate, olives, and other appetizers are a relief, as it's enough to be a dinner.

"I don't think I've ever made sourdough bread. Doesn't it take forever?"

Keats shrugs while he studies the set list of wines for tonight. "They mentioned something about already having the starter yeast. Tonight is the dough and baking part. Not sure what that means, but I'm just going to trust it."

I pinch his arm. "Using your hands to knead dough. I believe there is a sexy theory about hands and the ability to bake bread. You better prove the theory right."

"Except you've already felt my hands, so your theory has been solved." He pops an olive into his mouth.

"Do we get to take the bread home? And do I have to share? Because that might be a problem. My neighbor is dreadful."

Keats turns in his seat to face me fully. "Listen, my little demon, as much as pushing one another's buttons is our style, perhaps we can try another method of communication. A little more angelic, perhaps."

My fingertips begin to feather the back of his hand that is resting on the table, and we both observe my actions. "I would like that," I agree.

Our eyes meet, and we are both happy, having a good time, feeling the new direction of how we interact with one another. We almost get lost in the elation, but then Keats snaps out of it.

"Okay, bread-making. They said on the phone that we get to go home with sourdough starter, whatever the hell that means. Apparently, you need to take care of it like a plant. We get to mix the dough and knead it, and then they provide a different dough that's already risen," he explains.

I pick up the laminated sheet in front of us. "Wow, there are like a gazillion steps. This is what sophisticated bread does to us?"

"We can thank San Francisco for this. It's the sourdough capital of the world, apparently. Well, actually, Germany has the most consumption of sourdough bread. Although the Polish make some damn good stuff, too."

"Research much?"

He tries to hide his satisfied smile.

We order wine and a few minutes later, I'm picking up my glass of white wine, I take a sip. "Yum," I comment on the drink.

Keats also takes a sip of his wine, although he poured a much smaller glass for himself since he's driving. "I'm relieved you seem to be on board with tonight. I kind of noticed stuffy cocktail parties are not your thing and you prefer fields."

"I would say that I like to mix up my social calendar, but I do love nature for my daily outings. My heart is with wild fields and farm feels for engagement photos. There is a creek just out of town, and that's a great spot, too."

"Your face lights up when you talk about it."

I lift my shoulders. "It's a calming place. Is this when you tell me that bread-making is your calming zone?"

He has a deep chuckle. "Hell no. I can cook and grill, but baking is not my forte."

The waiter places a tray in front of us. We shuffle items around on the table to make space. With quick instructions, we get busy on mixing the ingredients.

My arm gives out mid-flour-mixing, and I collapse back into my seat. "Here. We need your muscle to finish this."

Keats takes over. "Your hero is here to assist."

The next hour we continuously laugh and joke around. It's constant switching what we produce with the staff who provide a new dough to keep the steps flowing.

We are at our last step where we are shaping the dough to put into a Dutch oven dish with all eyes on us due to our hysterics. While the bread is baking at a solid 450 degrees, we enjoy nibbles and drinks.

"I won't need to go to yoga for days. What a workout that was," I comment.

"But that smell from the kitchen is worth it. Do you prefer butter or olive oil on your bread?" he wonders.

"Hmm. Probably olive oil and mix that with a little balsamic and herbs. I'm sure we could steal a few from Mrs. Tiller's garden. The dog across the street eats her plants anyhow."

Keats brings his arm around me to rest on the back of my chair, and I can't help scooting a little closer to him. "Aren't you a little rebel," he responds.

Watching the people around us, it appears everyone seems to be on a date except the trio of girlfriends in the corner chatting about single life. Another reminder that I'm here with someone, and I like that a lot.

I nearly faint when the loaf of bread is brought to us. "Wait," I say and dive into my bag for my phone. "This deserves a photo."

Keats grins. "Okay, that makes sense. I need to send this to my sister, and then she will send a bunch of questions in return."

I elbow him in jest. "But you love it." I get a few shots, and then I hand the bread knife to Keats. "You may do the honors."

He's so laidback tonight, with ease remaining on his face the whole night. The bread's crust makes a crackly noise, and I nudge his arm with excitement.

"Ooh, this is nice and soft inside. Probably warm, too." He quickly winks at me, and I playfully roll my eyes.

Keats offers me a piece, and the first bite is nearly orgasmic, and I murmur a sound.

"I've heard that noise before," he teases.

"Well, aren't you funny." I rip off another piece while he brings his slice to his lips, I patiently wait for his reaction, and I cock an eyebrow. "I've seen that face before."

Not once has it crossed my mind to argue or throw a jab that is out of line, even for flirtation.

When our wine-and-loafs night wraps up, we head back to his car, but he doesn't start his engine. Instead, a promising quiet surrounds us, and the streetlights trace our faces. Our fingers interlace in the middle between our seats. This is a softer side between us, maybe a shock to my body, too. For the last few months, I would never have imagined this.

"I had a good time." His voice is tender, and it causes my body to grow sensitive in all the right places.

"Me too," I reply. Biting my bottom lip, I decide a simple

two-word answer isn't enough. "Actually, I forgot what it's like to go on a date."

At record speed he jumps in. "I hear ya."

Our hands float around one another. I scoff a laugh. "Turns out that I might be kind of happy that my dry spell is broken with you."

Keats leans his head to the side, and our eyes meet with a glow around us. "Ditto," he agrees.

"That's good, because the whole next-door-neighbor aspect kind of complicates things, and as much as it's been fun to plan each other's murders, it would be a hell of a lot more uncomfortable if tomorrow we had to see one another after a horrible date." I point out the potential predicament of our situation

"Good thing this wasn't horrible then."

I smile because he is right.

He dives in to kiss me, his hand finding the spot behind my head to pull me closer to him. Our tongues flick, and our kiss grows deeper. This is completely different. Lust hasn't taken over us, instead it's a desire to explore more of this thing between us.

I murmur from the back of my throat as he steals another breath from me with a damaging kiss that is a confirmation more than domination. And when we barely part, he gingerly sucks and drags along my bottom lip. Our noses nuzzle; what the hell? I'm nuzzling my nose with Keats? This is my life right now?

I approve.

"Esme, I haven't told you something yet."

Is this where everything goes pop?

"You are so unforgivingly beautiful that it makes me crazy. You were exquisite as my mistress and stunning when you are a mess on the floor. I'm not sure why I've waited to tell you."

Smiling against his mouth for one last soft kiss, we retreat our heads back and our eyes linger. "What are the chances you can risk a speeding ticket? You must know a judge or something to get out of it, right?"

"Say no more." But before he even gets to turn the engine on, his cell begins to vibrate. "Sorry, I need to take this in case it's Summer. Bo has chickenpox."

"Of course." And let me drool because that is so endearing.

Keats, however, sighs. His face tightens, and he answers. "What is it, Oliver?" *Oh.* "Are you kidding me? Now? He's ready to sign now at 11pm instead of earlier when this should have gone down at 4pm?" I can only vaguely hear the other end of the call. "Oliver, I swear I'm about to strangle... Yeah, I know... Okay. Yep."

The moment Keats hangs up and looks at me with a pained face, my mood drops.

"I wish so much that this isn't happening, but a player from another team that we've been trying to nab has finally agreed to sign before he has to renew with his team tomorrow. They need the contract since there is a sharp deadline."

I frown. "Right."

He leans in to steal another kiss. "I'm sorry. This isn't how this was supposed to go... at all."

Taking a deep breath, I can hear the remorse in his voice. I force myself to smile, and in truth, I do understand, though I'm still disappointed. "I get it. It's... fine."

"It's not. But yeah, I need to take you home, and it seems my night will be long in a way I don't particularly want."

"Really, don't worry." I wave him off.

Keats shakes his head. "You're not going to attack me

again for not fucking your brains out after an evening together?"

I ease and even snicker a laugh. "I wasn't going to attack you… per se. Anyhow, no. You have my word that I will not repeat my past transgressions."

He gives me another quick kiss. "I'm sorry."

"I know you are. It just means you will have to make an even better impression on our second date."

Keats growls. "A second date, eh? Sounds promising."

"So it seems."

And something inside me flickers from the thought.

13
KEATS

I don't hate my job, but right now, I kinda hate my job.

It was a long night, but I survived like always. Needing fresh air, I decide that maybe a run is in order. Maybe that sounds crazy, but I'm on an adrenaline high, and normally it wakes me up. Grabbing my running shoes from the basket next to the front door, I slip into them and glance at my watch that says 11am. In an ideal world, I would be waking up with a woman in my bed, but that was not in Esme's and my cards last night.

Closing the front door behind me, I inhale a deep breath of fresh air on this sunny day.

Except it seems that today will be anything but shiny.

In the corner of my eye, I spot a hellbent Esme storming my way.

"You!" she snarls.

Oh man.

"Yes?"

"I'm so angry."

Scratching my cheek, I point out the obvious. "I'm so

confused. I thought you said that you wouldn't be angry that we didn't consummate our date that was going pretty well."

Her arms splay out in the direction of the driveway. "That was before you decided to ruin my driveway."

My eyes squinch to examine what she could possibly mean. Maybe I'm still too groggy for this all, but I'm not catching on.

"The sand," she snipes. "The fucking sand."

Ah crap, I see it now. Piles of sandbags.

"I'm going to guess they got delivered to the wrong address."

"No, really? Could have fooled me." She stands in her traditional stance, hand on her tipped-out hip.

I groan up to the sky. "I'm sorry."

"Who the hell orders sand?" she squeaks.

Stepping forward, I raise my palms in an attempt to calm her. "It's supposed to be for the sandbox in my backyard. I wanted to make a play area for my nephew when he visits."

For a millisecond, her eyes soften, and I'm sure I just gained a point from the less-pissed version of Esme. That's the power of little kids and hot guys. Except...

"Sand? Really?" Her voice pipes up. "You realize that it's the worst possible thing you could do. A swing would probably be better. But *no,* someone wants to make their life complicated by inviting sand to get freaking everywhere in their house."

She doesn't appreciate the grin now on my face. "One, why do you care about my house? And two, sand is educational, he can build things with it."

Esme continues to glare at me. "Get the sand off my driveway," she gripes. "I don't have time for this. I need to get to a shoot then dinner with Hailey."

"And calm down a bit," I add on, one-toned.

Her eyes gawk at me, and she jabs her finger into my chest. "Don't be cute right now."

My grin stays tight. "I will fix it, okay. Now, can we sweep this under the rug?"

"Sweep it off my driveway," she deadpans.

"That too."

We both pause, and I take my chances by touching her shoulder. "Don't want to talk about last night?" Her face doesn't flinch, but her eyes have a glint of joy. "No? Too soon?"

"Move. The. Sand."

I'm trying not to laugh, but Esme is too freaking adorable because I can tell she would rather we rip one another's clothes off right now. I've come to learn her body language now that I've been inside her a few times.

I see the signs of a smile on her lips creeping through, but before she commits to showing me, she walks away, not even looking back. "Better be gone before I get back," she reminds me. I can tell by the tone that she's grinning to herself.

"A pleasure as always," I call out.

She's exhilarating, that one.

My eyes shift to the sand pile, and I sigh.

Shit. That's going to be a pain in the ass to move.

Liam and Oliver both have blank faces as I just finished explaining the last 24 hours. We're sitting outside on Oliver's deck, and he pauses as he cuts into a steak.

"You two are a little strange, not going to lie. The hot-and-cold thing is kind of exhausting even to watch," he mentions then takes the plunge into dishing up some salad.

"Very true. I thought we were going in the right direction,

then this morning she returned to being Godzilla. I kind of thought our new unidentified state would mean we could talk in a civil way, but apparently not. The saving grace is that she desperately wanted to smile."

Liam chuckles as he flips off the cap of another beer. "You two love the back-and-forth."

"Could be a problem then, because mellow us might not be compatible."

"Or you could be even better. You might end up with a ring on your finger, too," he replies.

Oliver offers me the salad bowl. "Liam might be biased since he is in a cloud of pre-wedding adventures that his fiancée drags him through. He doesn't know how to answer," he jokes.

"Oh yeah? Then what do you think?" I face Oliver.

A smirk draws on Oliver's mouth. "That you've been pining for Esme for months. And for a man who is glued to his job, then *boom*, now you are finding that maybe you can balance it all. Heaven forbid you have a woman who waits for you and can send you in surprise directions. Keeps you on your toes, just like a deadline."

"Seriously, get a girlfriend, and then I won't have to hear your philosophy. I hear Liam has a sister." I give Oliver a fake smile because I know that bugs him.

"Nuh-uh. My sister is off-limits," Liam reminds us both.

Oliver clears his throat. "Of course, I'm just waiting for a crazy neighbor. I knew I should have brought the house up the street. I could be closer to daily entertainment."

Tossing the salad in the serving bowl, I highlight the obvious. "Look, I will let this all play out. It's new, and it's been a while since I've been off the market. My sister is insistent that a wife and kid are on my horizon, and she prefers if it's sooner than later."

"You have sourdough starter in a jar in your kitchen. Trust me, you're on your road to marriage," Oliver comments.

That causes me to laugh. "Anyhow, I should have this weekend off since we pulled a late one last night. I shall test the waters again with Esme. I'm fairly confident that she really was just pissed off about the sand, which is fair enough."

"Well, I would be also. Sandbags are hell to carry." Liam takes a drink from his beer.

"I know. It replaced my run, and I'm positive my arms will hurt tomorrow."

We all get comfortable at the table. It's great that Oliver lives so close. It makes meetups easy.

"Admittedly, I do have difficulty seeing you domesticated, but Esme isn't your typical woman, and besides, I need her in your life so I can get another pie."

My eyes whip to Oliver. "You got a pie, too?"

He shrugs as though I'm crazy. "Of course. She makes one for everyone on the street when they move in or have a special life event. Not my fault you got on her shit list. You bad boy you." Now he's just provoking me.

Liam laughs at our friend's humor.

"Can we please switch topics? For example, who will host the Fourth of July BBQ?" It's an insanely busy time for me, with free agency having started on July first and players needing to be locked down before next season. In work terms, it isn't a great time for hosting duties, but I guess I'll be able to breathe for a hot second.

"Not me," Liam is quick to answer.

Oliver doesn't answer, instead giving me the look that it will be me, and I sigh. "Fine. I'll do it. But one of you has to bring the beer."

"Deal. We'll just have to keep our phones on standby."

Oliver nods. "Alright, boys, eat up as we have the finals highlights to watch. No more mention of those who shall not be named."

Finally.

We didn't make it a long night. In fact, it's only nine, but whoa, it's been a long day, and I'm exhausted. A good night of sleep is in order. Shutting my laptop down, I just leave it on the coffee table since tomorrow morning I'll probably need to reply to a work email. My bad.

My nose tingles, and with one sniff, I smell something. Is that smoke?

Huh. I didn't use anything today that would cause smoke. I double-check my phone charger, and then in the kitchen, but I don't see anything. The smell is getting stronger.

Hearing people outside, I walk to my living room window, and then I see it.

Shit.

Esme's house.

Not a second goes by before I'm running out of my house to the street where everyone is congregating. My eyes search for the issue, but the bright glow from the fire on the side of the house speaks for itself.

The side of Mrs. Tiller's house is on fire, and it seems to have spread to Esme's house.

Esme.

Panic and alarm hit me, and I crane my neck in a desperate search. She can't be in her house. Esme would have noticed right away and gotten out. A smoke detector would work. It has to work.

My stomach and chest do a flip in unison. Where is Esme?

Only a slither of relief comes to me when I see Esme driving up. Thank God, she had her shoot then dinner with Hailey, I remember her mentioning it.

I'm not even sure she bothers to turn the engine off when she parks because she doesn't close her car door and terror fills her eyes.

For a second she stands motionless as she grasps what is happening, and time stands still while the sound of sirens approaching mix with the fire blazing. It doesn't matter that in my peripheral view, Mrs. Tiller is weeping in our neighbor Kelly's arms. Shock wears off Esme's face, and horror kicks in.

"My pictures," she yells right before she begins to run toward the fire. I don't waste time before I'm after her, grabbing her from behind, pretty much tackling her. She wiggles in my arms, desperate to escape. "I have to go in there."

Falling to the ground, I grip her arms tight to her body, and I huddle around her from behind, pulling her as close as humanly possible. "No."

"Let me go," she cries out.

"Not a fucking chance." I grind my words out into her ear. I'm not even sure she realizes whose arms she is in, as she's focused on the scene before her.

She repeatedly tries to push me away to no avail. "No."

Her struggle causes me to loop my arms around her chest to hold her down with more restraint. "Listen to me. You can't go in there, I won't let you."

Esme sobs, and I feel her entire body fall into a thousand pieces.

I kiss her hair and begin to rock her gently in my arms, as

if that would actually calm her; it won't, especially as the fire department arrives.

"I'm not letting you go," I whisper into her ear. I have no clue if she even hears me as disbelief takes over her body from the scene before her, but if she understands anything, then she would know…

I mean every word.

14

KEATS

Testing the bath water, I decide it's the right temperature. My clawfoot tub was a luxury the designer said was needed to fit in with the checkered tile and feel of the old house. I've never used it, though.

Turning off the faucet, I stare at Esme who is sitting on a stool, mute, with a glass of whiskey in hand. She looks nearly lifeless. Completely deflated and heartbroken. Maybe still in shock. A mixture of it all, and still she let me guide her away.

It took a few hours to put out the fire. Afterward, we listened to the firefighter explain the situation. Apparently, Mrs. Tiller forgot to replace an old toaster, and it short-circuited. The firemen were able to extinguish the fire, but the smoke and charred house remain. Luckily, only the kitchen and living room in Esme's house have been destroyed, and not everything. Even more important, Esme wasn't in the house.

She's exhausted, and I've forgotten that I was already lacking sleep from the day before.

"Come on, let's get you in the tub." I walk on my knees to her and set her whiskey on the sink vanity before I begin to help her undress. First her blouse, and then I tug her jeans off as her legs part open. Reaching around her, I unhook her bra. Everything smells of smoke, and there is no way she can put these back on.

"It's gone." She's motionless. I help her up and into the tub. I'm about to leave her for a second to search underneath my sink for hotel bubble bath or anything remotely usable for the tub. Esme grabs my wrist. "Don't leave me."

"Just grabbing soap," I assure her.

Finding a small bottle and grabbing a washcloth, I return to her as she stares blankly forward. I pour the small bottle and hang the cloth on the rim of the tub. Peeling my shirt up and off, I strip down and step into the warm water to sit behind her, positioning myself so she's between my legs.

Immediately she leans into me. "All my photos."

"Shh, don't worry about that now." I kiss her neck, and the overpowering smell of fire is drenched in her hair. I begin to comb the strands with my wet hands. As much as Esme has backups of everything she photographs, my guess is she means the photos from when she was younger on the wall.

"I feel so numb."

Wetting the washcloth, I begin to scrub her arms, going slowly and gently. I'm not even second-guessing taking care of her now. It's pure instinct.

"Try and relax. There is nothing you can do right now."

I give up on the need for suds to spread over our bodies and instead rest with Esme. Her fingers skim the surface of the water, and I kiss her shoulder. We don't need to say anything; tonight's events are enough to occupy our brains.

"I'm so tired." Nothing that she says has any tone, only somberness.

Stroking her arms, I want to comfort her, and I'm not sure if I'm doing this all right. "It will be okay."

She tips her head up, attempting to glance over her shoulder. "Maybe in this moment it is. I fear for tomorrow."

"You don't need to. I'm here."

Esme nestles further into my body, and we're a fit perfect for this tub.

"I won't wake up tomorrow and find this was a nightmare, will I?"

Rubbing her arms with my hands, I reply, "I can't promise that. But I hope being here in the water with me isn't a nightmare." I try to make her smile, and when I do my best to curve my head around her body to check, I see a very faint stretch of her lips, and that's good enough for me.

We stay this way for quite a while, just lying in the tub, and I clean her with the cloth. When the water cools and we both smell of peppermint from the soap, I get out and wrap a towel around my waist and bring the other up and open wide to wrap around her when she stands.

Now isn't the time to admire how beautiful she is completely naked. I need to get her warm.

In my room, I give her one of my shirts to sleep in, and she leads her own way into my bed, pulling the duvet up. She's intent on sleeping. If she's like me then her body must feel weighted down.

Staying in my boxer briefs, I opt not to wear a shirt because I will just get too warm. Joining her in bed, I scoop her protectively in my arms until her head is tucked under my chin. I gently reach to turn the light off.

To my dismay, she rolls out of my arms and lies on her side. Mirroring her position, we face one another, and I kiss her forehead. "Try and sleep," I whisper.

Her only answer is to peek her head out to kiss my lips. A chaste kiss, a parting before sleep kicks in.

But I'm mistaken as she hooks her leg over me, and with

her in only my shirt and nothing else, I realize that I should have offered her shorts, too.

It doesn't matter, as she wants one thing, and she rubs her body against me. "Please," she murmurs.

This is what she needs now.

Maybe I should question her on this, but she's already reaching between us to slip her hand inside my boxer briefs. This is how people sometimes deal with grief, and I'll give her this.

I begin to trail my fingers up her legs, smooth from the bath. Esme scoots my briefs down until my cock springs free, already hard. Her legs part open, and I swipe my fingers between them to feel how much she wants this.

I move to enable me to bring my mouth to her pussy, discarding my underwear in the process. Lying on my stomach, I push the fabric of my shirt up to reveal her breasts. Spreading kisses from her bellybutton up, I slow the journey up to take a nipple in my mouth, and I hear a gentle gasp. Gently squeezing her tits with my palms, I remind myself that she is fragile glass right now.

Which is why I abandon her breasts and retrace the road of my kisses and move down, pausing just above her pubic bone, and her hips tilt up, offering me more.

"You're so beautiful," I utter softly against her skin, and I drag my lips along the line of her hipbone.

Esme has a shaky breath but sinks her nails into my hair to guide me lower, as she knows exactly what she wants.

Immediately, I give her clit an open-mouthed kiss, and she cries out my name. Sucking, I swirl the tip of my tongue, and her hips swivel. How have I not taken more time to worship her this way before? Lapping her up, I'm addicted and want more. When she begins to ride my mouth, I follow her cues and take over the rhythm she wants and pin her hips down to keep her still against the mattress.

Esme needs to relax, and that means I will give that to her. I could get lost in doing this for her. I want to make her come until she's in such a state that she'll fall blissfully asleep.

Exploring her, I drive my tongue within her for a quick taste, and her moan is soft but effective for me to be encouraged that I'm getting just the right spot. But she doesn't give me a chance to go deeper as she is guiding me to slither up her body to kiss her lips.

"Please," she quietly pleads.

Her hand glides between us to guide my tip to her entrance, and I slide right in. Taking her with me, I lie on my side and move inside her with her leg hooked over my hip. It gives me a better position to hug her close, and Esme is intent on framing my face with her hands while I thrust deeper inside of her.

We are on overload, our bodies extra sensitive, grinding a rhythm together. Every light kiss sends electric currents through our bodies, every hard pump cementing us closer to being inseparable, and my hand on her hip keeps her down so she doesn't float away because that's what it feels like; we're not on this earth. Or rather, we're forgetting about where we are.

She nips my shoulder and encases tighter around my cock. We sync together, and our breaths grow heavy. This isn't like what we've done before. It's more intimate and maybe even confronting, because this doesn't feel like a game.

No words leave us as we chase our release, with no chance of slowing down, either. Only when she begins to tremor in my arms, letting a heaving sigh of calm leave her lips, and her body relaxing all around me, do I allow my own relief. I fill her up, not at all bothered that she'll be marked with me for the rest of the night.

Because when I roll to my back and she tucks into my body, I know she has no plans on leaving this bed.

I brush her hair with my fingers as she listens to my pulse beating extra hard, and her fingers feather over my chest. She is clinging to me, and that's completely the way it should be.

"Close your eyes, Esme," I murmur against her hair and plant my lips on the top of her head.

"Just stay like this until I fall asleep." I can hear the fatigue in her voice, but her breath has evened out.

"I'll give you whatever you want." I'm not even sure she heard me because I'm not certain that thought left my mouth.

But it's true.

And as she drifts to sleep in my arms, having let me take care of her all night, I realize something else.

There is more meaning underlying my statement.

I have feelings for her. I'm not just the guy helping her tonight. I'm the guy who wants to protect her and the man who won't let her walk away.

15

ESME

My entire head is a brick, and my body aches, which is why it's odd that I also feel rested at the same time. The sleepy slumber that I'm in as I wake up is almost peaceful. Only accentuated by the fact that the pillows and mattress feel heavenly.

Vaguely, I hear Keats's voice, and he seems to be in the hall near the bedroom door. "Just move around my schedule. I doubt I'll be in Monday morning," he speaks in a thin yet clipped tone before he must hang up.

Yawning, I begin to wiggle my body as he patters into his room.

"Hey, there you are, sleepyhead." His content tone feels false, probably because of how I ended up here.

I rub my eyes as I sit up, noticing that I'm wearing Keats's shirt. Oh yeah, because my clothes stink of smoke.

This is my life? Gone up in flames?

"Tell me it was all a dream."

He winces. "I wish I could." Keats comes to sit on the side of the bed near me.

Am I still in shock or has reality set in? One glance to

Keats who is dressed yet kept a little stubble on his chin, his eyes glazed with concern and pity, and I know that shock is long over.

"What time is it?" I wonder, as I can see the sun is bright outside where he partly opened his curtains.

He touches my arm as he sits and comfort spreads through me. "You were tired, so I didn't wake you, but it's almost ten."

"Wow. That's probably the only miracle. I slept." I'm lacking energy in my voice.

"It could have been worse," he reminds me.

Thinking about it for a few moments, I guess he is right. "At least, my camera equipment and laptop were in my car, since I was away for a shoot earlier in the day. It's just my…"

"House," he finishes my sentence.

Silence grows in the room, eerily relaxing.

This man. How does he have abilities that I've never seen before? He's supportive, and it's a bonus that he's easy on the eyes. Something positive for the day.

Maybe it's hysteria due to last night, but I snort out a laugh and begin to chuckle to myself. Keats watches me peculiarly.

"What's funny?"

Flopping back onto my pillow, I slide along the mattress to rest on my side and observe him. "I've never seen your room. It's always been doors and floors as our settings of choice."

Now he smirks, too. "You forgot about the table."

Exploring the room with my eyes, there are a lot of grays happening, but the large windows make up for it. I bring my hand to run along the mattress. "Nice bed."

"Thanks for your approval." He lifts his feet up and joins me on his side.

"If I recall, I was angry at you yesterday."

Keats wraps a few strands of hair around his finger to touch me affectionately. "Long forgotten. Besides, you were pissed at me for not letting you run into a burning house, too. If I were to keep a scoreboard then you are really racking up points. Lucky for you, that too is long history."

I swoop his finger away only to bring it to my lips for a little peck. "Truthfully, it's all a little blurry what happened, but thank you for saving me, and I do remember being with you."

Keats licks his lips, his smile sudden. "Did you just say thank you to me?" he teases.

"Yes," I reply bluntly.

"Noted. Now, as much as I wish you could sleep, you need to get out of my bed."

My brows furrow. "Kicking me out of bed already?"

He shakes his head and leaves the mattress. "No. But we have to deal with insurance and assess the damage. Not to mention, we need the details from Mrs. Tiller's insurance."

Kicking the duvet further toward the foot of the bed, I swing my feet to the ground and rub my head when I stand. "What exactly happened again?"

Keats is rummaging in his drawer when he answers. "According to Sheriff Carter—"

"Again, why can't everyone just say Carter? He's our neighbor."

"And a sheriff who had words with the fire department, so…"

I look at him plainly.

"Something in the toaster in Mrs. Tiller's house went wrong. Hopefully it's mostly smoke damage to your home. She's at the hospital for a checkup. With her old age, even unscathed, a double-check was needed. Her daughter is driving down from Michigan to help sort everything out."

I begin to pace and try to digest all the details. "What a nightmare."

He tosses clothes onto the bed. "Like I said, it could have been worse. Here. Your clothes from yesterday are in the washing machine, so you will need something else to wear. Hailey called, and she will bring you some clothes later."

Wearing his shirt isn't bad at all, but having normal clothes for public outings is ideal. Nonetheless, I snatch up one of his button-downs, and if I were brave enough, I could wear it as a dress, but it's just a shade too risqué for the neighborhood.

"There is a spare toothbrush and things in the bathroom." Looking at him strangely, he must understand my mind. "Relax, I have a bunch of hotel kits from traveling. If you feel the need to destress with sewing, then there is probably a thread with a spare button in there, too."

"Sewing isn't for me, and thank you again."

Keats circles the bed with a strong stride to stand before me and raises his hands to frame my face with my hair between his fingers. The hold he has on me is firm which makes it easy for him to lower his lips to mine for a deep kiss. One that I'm receptive to, anchoring me down on earth and creating longing for this man that I no longer view as an enemy. Keats is a man of character and caring. Just so happens, I'm lucky enough that he wants to be those things with me. I kiss him back, powerful and confirming. I don't want to run away. Even when I want to shut myself away from the world right now, I want to do that with him.

We part, and he kisses my forehead delicately. "It will be okay," he promises.

Our eyes meet for a mutual agreement. If they could talk, then it would be to say that he'll protect me, and I'll let him.

Eyes always speak the truth.

Walking through the rubble with Keats, the smell of smoke means that we will need to shower when we get back to his place. We can see the remnants of part of my house. Or rather, we can see the kitchen and living room, but there is a giant black hole.

"Luckily, it didn't spread upstairs," he highlights.

"I should be grateful for that, but my entire kitchen and living room are gone. Nothing is savable here."

Keats gently kicks a piece of burnt wood while his hands stay in his pockets. "They need to check the foundation and the load-bearing walls for upstairs. The insurance guy mentioned he will get out here only on Monday. I'll talk to him about getting some temporary beams in."

I grab his arm to give us a pause. "Wait... I heard you earlier that you're not working on Monday. Is it..." There is no way. He never abandons work.

"You need help with this." He downplays this, but it means a lot to me.

"You don't have to do that. I know you're busy," I assure him. His lips press together, clearly disagreeing, and it's apparent that there is no point debating this. Besides, my heart warms over this gesture, and that's a feeling I don't want to let go of. "Thank you."

We take a few more steps into my home. "My desk sanctuary. My photos. The flowers you gave me. Hell, even my pie plates... all gone," I list in a daze.

Keats nudges my arm with his elbow. "They are all

replaceable. Besides, your pie plates were not really being used to their full potential since I never got a baked present."

I flash my eyes at him, grateful that he is trying to make this easier on me, but I need to keep this appraisal going. "Upstairs will need to be aired out for what feels like forever. Re-painted, too. Maybe new flooring in my bedroom because it's above the kitchen. Probably just better to start all over again."

"I'm not sure what to say except… it could have been worse, and lucky for all of us, you are still standing here."

I rest my head on his upper arm as we stand side by side. "Lucky us," I echo.

It's a long minute of staring at the scene until I sigh and decide that we've seen enough. There is nothing I can do today.

I interlink my hand with Keats's as we exit my charred home. We notice a woman helping Mrs. Tiller out of the front seat of her car. That must be her daughter.

"Oh, Esme. I'm so sorry," she wails.

Swallowing my anger, I remember that it was an accident. I mosey her way with Keats in tow. "How are you feeling?" My hand creates a visor over my eyes due to the sunlight.

"I'm too strong. Nothing is wrong. But your house…" she cries. In the corner of my eye, Keats is shaking hands with Mrs. Tiller's daughter.

"Your house, too."

Her daughter interrupts. "I've called the insurance company, and I will be sure to keep you updated."

That headache is returning, and Keats must notice. "I think today we just focus on the shock."

We all study each other with solemnity and complete deflation. The shining sun does fuck all to lighten the mood.

It's a little chitchat more before Keats and I head back to his house, and he ushers me to the kitchen.

"Hey, look at that, you have a working kitchen," my humor is a little cynical today.

He smiles to himself, amused. "A saving grace because you need to be fed. Besides, I'm starving. Being a superhero is hard work. It gets me the girl, but it's a killer on my physique," he jokes.

"I need donuts and coffee."

"Oliver is stopping by soon. "

"Hailey, too," I say.

We both blink our eyes and then give one another a knowing smile. Those two.

While we wait, Keats makes me a coffee with his fancy machine, and although it's downright delicious, it isn't Foxy Rox coffee. I've finished one round when I hear Oliver let himself in.

"I'm here with supplies," he calls out from the front door and heads straight for the kitchen, balancing a box of donuts and a tray of coffees.

"Thanks." I don't look up to acknowledge him because I'm sedated with grief, not trying to be rude.

Oliver places the box on the counter and opens the lid, quick to offer me one. Oh great, a chocolate old-fashioned with glaze, because that will really save my day… Okay, it's ten seconds of happiness, but still.

"Sorry about your house. Everyone on the street has been talking about it. My run was basically start and stop as everyone wanted to share their concerns, except true to Everhope Road, it was more about who is starting the casserole calendar."

Keats bubbles a laugh. "Just what we all need. A thousand casseroles and Mrs. Callings' mint fudge."

Oliver raises his hand. "Whoa, if you are getting mint fudge then bring it my way."

They have banter, and it's refreshing to hear, but even they grow quiet when they realize the circumstances of why we are all sitting in Keats's kitchen eating donuts at one in the afternoon. Breakfast is late today for reasons out of my control.

"As great as Oliver is for Foxy Rox deliveries, I actually asked him here because insurance policies are more his thing, so he can have a look or figure out what to do," Keats explains.

I offer them both a weak sign of approval.

"Hi." A familiar female voice is heard. "Can I just come in?" I guess Hailey has been here before since her brother is Keats's friend.

"Yeah," Keats calls out.

Before I know it, my friend's arms are engulfed around me for a big hug. "I can't believe this. How crazy. Luckily, you are safe."

"I know." I shake out my body, hands included. "Knew that house was cursed, damn it. I guess it's now a good thing I never got that cat. That would have been a travesty," I quip.

Hailey's face is blank. "I appreciate that you haven't lost your funny bone. But wow... I have some extra clothes in the car, and when you stay with me then we'll make space for your laptop and stuff."

I huff out a breath. "The few things that were saved, yippee," I add dryly. "And that reminds me that I have clients I need to reschedule."

"She's staying here." All of our attentions whip to Keats who has been quietly listening yet just spoke up, his voice unwavering.

Oliver and Hailey both stare oddly at one another as my eyes connect with Keats's.

"Excuse me?"

"You're staying here." Keats crosses his arms, standing firm, and something about this view irks me and also tingles me in all the right places.

I scoff a sound. "Ludicrous."

He shakes his head side to side once, with his eyes not lingering off track with mine. "No, it's not."

I take one step forward and straighten my spine. "Really?" I doubt him.

"Uh, I think Oliver and I will head to the living room," Hailey states awkwardly, her face soured.

"Why? This could be fun." Oliver is game to be a bystander to the rage building inside of me, even if it isn't rage at all, or at least not the negative kind. He even breaks off a piece of a donut for snacks.

Hailey lurches to her side and grabs his arm. "Read the room, Oliver, read the room. We do not stay to witness this." She yanks his arm.

It wouldn't matter what they do, as Keats and I are both pulling on an invisible rope for a game of tug-of-war.

"I don't think you want to stay with Hailey."

My nose tips up, not sure what words just hit my ear. "W-what?"

"Stay here." Is he offering or demanding? Either way, determination runs strong, and it feels like a giant safety net wrapping around me.

"Again, what?" My eyes flutter in astonishment that he is persistent.

Keats steps closer, heat building between us. "You can stay here, and I don't think you want to leave."

"You have some audacity to assume." I think I've unconsciously added a dare underneath that sentence. A challenge to him to debate this because I fear that I want to walk into his arms, breathe him in, and surrender to his demand.

He smirks, and his thumb brings my lips together before his fingerprint caresses my lips. "Stay." The man seems unaffected by everything I say.

"Look." I step back to break our contact. "Thank you for last night, really. You were a comfort or are or… but one night in your bed doesn't mean that I can just move in. That's crazy."

He cocks his head to the side. "Is it, though? You'll be able to check in next door whenever you want."

"I'll be stuck with you," I deadpan, and my body begins to let a molecule-sized smile form.

"The guy you've been kind of liking lately."

My eyes enlarge at the reminder. "Moving in is a little more than how a normal second date should go."

Keats lets out a sinister scoff. "I don't think it's our second. Are we counting last night? Every time we were together before?"

Now I beam. "See? That's the reminder that hate sex was kind of our thing. We'll argue a lot."

Keats closes our distance to grip my lower arms and raise them up slightly. "I'm up for the challenge, are you?"

Am I thinking clearly? Or does Keats see right through me and presses the button of my honesty? Because I'm intrigued by his offer. It's crazy and exciting.

Time to be practical, though. "I can't inconvenience you, and besides, I really need to remind us one more time that we were insufferable with one another. Granted…" My brows furrow. "The tide has been changing—"

"I'm not worried. Stay." It's a repeated request but also subconsciously prods the truth of what I might want.

I squint as I study his endearing face. Geez, is this what people have to deal with when he's negotiating a contract? My sight draws down to his hands holding me firm. I recall everything he's already done.

I can't help but wonder. "Why do you care so much?" I ask in a rasp, hopeful of his answer.

The corner of his mouth snags tight. "Everyone deserves someone, no matter their history. Turns out you're my someone, and maybe I'm your someone too."

His answer steals my words, leaving me speechless. Why does it feel profound and promising?

Trapping my bottom lip with my teeth, I decide not to prolong the discussion and instead fold his proclamation and tuck it down into my body for a later time.

My grimace returns when I think of a point that I should highlight if I'm agreeing to this scenario. "This doesn't mean we'll be having sex all the time." A total lie just flew out of my mouth, but I attempt to simmer down our thoughts that probably have floated in once or twice in this conversation.

Keats licks his bottom lip, tenacious yet clearly not bothered by my words. "Huh," is all he says, and it's unnerving. "Esme, you're not going anywhere, just accept that. Besides, I don't think you want to leave."

"That's clearly a mandate." I blow out a breath that transforms my desire to dispute into approval. Ah, what the hell. My house is in rubble, and I could use an adventure. I nod subtly in agreement. "You're right." Satisfied, he drops my arms in turn for his hand cupping my cheek. "I don't think I want to leave."

"Then don't."

Poof. Any signs of the brief tense conversation we had vanishes.

He kisses me, wrapping me around his finger, as maybe

I'm too submissive, but honestly, there are no doubts inside me. In fact, I'm awakening.

"That means we have to deal with one another not arguing all the time," I whisper as I'm in a mesmerized state.

His facial expression is almost hungry. "Challenge accepted."

Nibbling my bottom lip, I don't mull long because we've been on a rollercoaster lately, but over the last 24 hours, he's helped me ensure I don't receive lasting emotional trauma that might leave a wound. "Seems... agreement is in our cards," I answer.

"It's settled then," he proudly confirms.

Keats's tiny grin is errant, and most of all, his eyes promise that he won't let me fall into a thousand pieces.

"Are you sure?" Hailey says as she hands me the bag from her car. We managed to take an hour for all of us to eat some donuts and drink coffee. Any talk related to my house was with an optimistic direction.

"Yeah. Besides, it will be easier to deal with the house."

She shrugs at me. "Okay, just..." She starts to laugh. "Look at you two. Who would have thought... Oh yeah, I did." Hailey seems proud of herself, and a closed-mouth smile remains on my face.

I glance off into the distance, down the street where a few kids are playing with a remote-control car. "It's not like that."

"Sure." She isn't convinced.

I bring my gaze back to her. "Would you like me to throw in Oliver's name right now or will you behave?"

The shade of irritation on her face is immediate. "Fine. I won't bother you about Keats."

Holding up the bag, I say, "Thank you. I'll call you tomorrow. I might be living at Foxy Rox to avoid facing my nearly-burnt-down house."

Her lips pucker out. "Or I can just highlight that you are living here."

"Temporarily."

"Okay. Right." She doesn't seem to believe me. "Anyhow, you two kids have fun. I need to head to dinner at my brother's."

We hug goodbye, and I don't even bother stealing a look at my house, it's just too depressing.

When I'm inside, I vaguely hear Oliver giving Keats the same third degree as I got outside. "You two do what you want, but you kind of look like shit. When was the last time you slept normally?"

"A while. I was already lacking due to work, and then this happened."

Keats's saccharine side is almost too soft for me. He hasn't slept mostly due to me, but he hasn't complained.

Stepping into the living room, Oliver gives me a smile when he walks by to leave. "Good luck, Esme. But you're in good hands." He isn't even taunting me, he's being sincere.

With everyone gone, I slowly walk to Keats like prey as he attempts to clean up the coffee table.

Reaching my destination, I touch his hand to stop him. Instead, I set the empty mug in his hand back down on the surface.

"I'll do that later, but I think we are both tired and could use a little sleep." He more than deserves that.

His lips roll in for a second. "Perhaps a little true."

I offer my hand. "Come on. We can discuss bedmate rules later."

He shakes his head to himself, perhaps in awe that I'm

doing my best to brighten my spirits, and it's a struggle, but I'll try.

I tow Keats along behind me upstairs. The moment we are in his room, he's already stripping his shirt up and off with full intention to sleep, but I have another plan. A coping method that seems to work for me.

Pushing him onto his bed, he's slightly taken aback but lets me lead with intrigue.

I'm overcome with a powerful need to take control, which is why I straddle his shirtless body. The way his eyes travel up my body is enough for him.

I don't want to think about anything in the outside world. He can be my escape today.

"What is this?" He doesn't sound disappointed at all.

My fingers wrap around the edges of his t-shirt that's been on me since after I changed again. I didn't bother changing into Hailey's clothes because I would rather have Keats's scent all over me. Lifting the shirt, he gets the clue right away, and his eyes direct straight to my chest.

"We never actually get fully naked around one another, and I don't particularly want to talk right now," I inform him.

His devilish grin causes an ache around my clit. I unbuckle his belt, and the click of the clasp breaking free is a sound I enjoy. It means we are closer to our destination.

Right now, I want to land between his legs with my mouth on him.

"What do you have in mind, Esme?" Keats clucks his tongue.

I kiss his chest then place popcorn kisses down and going lower. "Something I haven't yet done with you," I taunt.

One tug and his cock is free from clothing. I wrap my hand around the base, and with my eyes striking up to his, I ensure he watches when my tongue darts out and swirls around the head. Instantly, his cock twitches, but I don't give myself much chance to feel that against my lips as my mouth lowers down to sheathe him into my mouth.

"How have you waited to do this? And how have I not insisted to test your skills." He moans.

Popping my mouth off, I flick the tip of my tongue over his cock. "You can spank me for that later."

"Or I can punish you now." Keats moves his hands to my hair and quickly wraps everything around his hand with a little force, pulling me into the friction of his hand. He leads me to what he wants. "Take it as deep as you can. And then I will make sure you can take it even deeper after that."

Taking a deep breath, I do my best to take every inch of him inside my mouth, but Keats isn't small by any means. I already feel my gag reflex kicking in, and I swallow to tighten around his length and pump up. Keats presses me back down, true to his word.

He and I know one another's limits. That's the one thing that has always been our instant connection. We both like it a little rough and dirty, but I have trust that if I wanted it to stop that he instantly would. But right now? I want this. My mouth is watering, and my entire body is eager for him.

I suck and moan. Even when he is so deep that I feel tears forming in my eyes, I still love every second of this.

"You are excellent at taking my cock, Esme." His breath is heavy, and his enjoyment seeps through every word. "But I think we are two creatures who would prefer to come with your pussy full of my cock."

I nod and mumble as his cock is in my mouth, but he just expressed what he wants which is why I suck once more and slowly leave his cock.

Wiping my mouth with the back of my hand, my body is on fire and wants to be touched. When I climb up Keats's body, squaring his hips between my thighs, I'm grateful when his thumb begins to circle around my nub. Aligning him to my opening, I clamp down on him, drawing out both our moans.

Riding him a few times, he has other plans. He sits up, ensuring he stays inside me. My hands plant on his shoulders and his arms wind around my middle. If I let go then I'll just fall back onto the floor.

"Keep going," he whispers.

His mouth brushes hungrily along the slope of my neck, and I tense around his cock as my pussy and the sensitive tickle around my taut nipples connect. It raises sensitivity to the max. He twists a nipple between the pads of his fingers, while my hips rock every time I push down further to bring him as deep as possible.

Keats growls as he kisses up my neck before our mouths fuse for a long kiss. One that must bring out the side of him that's direct and in control. Proven by the fact he grips my hips and rolls us so I'm on my back.

"No way are you going to lead us. Those thighs of yours stay wide while I fill you up."

The blaze in his eyes brings out another whimper from me, and my body presses up because I need him close. The flames from the fire outside were less intense than inside with him.

We ignite together.

I'm not sure what tornado we create, but we both end up completely spent on top of his mattress. Two bodies tangled together.

"Now we sleep," he pants.

"Yes. You do need your beauty rest." How I manage to joke when I'm near breathless, I'm not sure.

Keats pulls me close until my head rests against his chest.

"Nah, the only beautiful thing is in my bed, and imagine that, I want her wrapped around my body."

Even red and warm, I blush. "Go to bed."

"Fine. Be warned I have no issue slipping into you when needed. If you're staying here, then I'm going to reap the benefits."

Smiling to myself, I like the sound of that.

I would say we are only interested in sex, except… he invited, or rather ordered, me into his home and has taken care of me.

And overnight, the sprinkles of more that were spreading between us over the last few weeks are now a trail of the past.

Because a profound urge to take another step between us has become irresistible and inevitable.

16

KEATS

This woman has me in a chokehold.
   I'm falling, or maybe I always have been, using our arguments as a ruse.

Stretching my arms, I yawn as I step down the stairs, the golden sun filling my house with light and the smell of bacon tingling my nose. To be honest, I'm still tired from this weekend, but this morning it's due to having Esme in my bed and our ability to mix adrenaline with sex to create a long night of epic proportions. We were supposed to sleep.

Arriving at the dining table, I pause, and my head lolls to the side as I study the head of the table. There's a plate with a folded newspaper resting on top of it. Cutlery nicely placed around the plate. There are those croissants from a canned roll of dough on a platter with a napkin underneath. Is that freshly squeezed orange juice?

Esme sings to herself. I hear her in the kitchen, and I guess we haven't actually slept overnight with one another until this weekend. This is her normal morning routine?

"You're up. Great, I was going to wake you for breakfast." Esme whizzes by me carrying a plate. She's wearing one of my work shirts and nothing else. My head tips a little more to get a view. Oh wait, there is a thong… I think.

Scratching my cheek, I'm trying to adjust to the scene. "Uh, what's this?"

She looks up to me with a bright smile as she sets the bacon down and adjusts the syrup bottle. "It's breakfast."

I slowly walk to my chair. "I can see that. It's just a little formal, don't you think?"

She is quick to meet me halfway and grabs my wrist to guide me faster to my seat. "Well, I remembered you mentioned about your Sunday paper and wanted to make sure you have a nice breakfast… a thank-you, really."

Smirking to myself, I feel a discussion coming. "Here I was thinking this is the new standard." I sit down.

Esme playfully pinches my arm before landing on her chair. "I just figured this is the least I could do." She begins to pour me coffee from the French press.

"I have a damn good machine in the kitchen."

She shrugs her shoulders. "But this is more fitting for the setting. It's all about atmosphere."

I sputter a laugh. "How am I to argue with the woman who literally has a room for her boudoir atmosphere."

Her smile remains but fades. "Well, it will be a while until it can be used again. It's okay, I have a lot of engagement shoots coming up, luckily." Her lips press together, and it's apparent she's soaking in her own mixed emotions. "So many things gone." Her voice trembles, but then she takes a deep breath through her nostrils and her eyes drift to the side. "I know it's only material, but still, a house can be your home, and now my home is like a piece of burnt toast." She deflates.

"Sourdough toast?" The corner of her mouth tugs weakly from my wit. Blowing out a deep breath, I know that I can't keep reiterating the obvious that all those things are items, but there is only one her. "You're here, and you're safe," is what I manage to come up with, and it's the truth.

Her eyes flick up to meet mine, and they're brimming with appreciation, and my heart constricts for a second, a warning perhaps. She's in front of me, in my home, in my shirt, and we're sharing breakfast. It's domesticated, and all that comes to mind is that this is the image that I can and want to get accustomed to.

"I'm safe because I'm here. Which brings me to our next point." Her serious thought is broken by her fingers snapping in the air. "Wait, I forgot to ask if you take sugar or milk in your coffee. I don't actually know. No, it's black, right? I recall mentioning that it's dark as your soul." She frowns in embarrassment.

"Memory lane, eh? And yes, black is fine."

Esme blows out a relieved exhale, and she seems to be psyching herself up. "So, our next item of discussion."

"For someone who makes fun of me for working too much, I wish to highlight that you seem to have a meeting agenda on a Sunday."

Her head bobs side to side. "It's just, if I'm going to be staying here for a little bit..." She holds her palm up. "I mean, it can't be that long. The insurance guy will give me more insight tomorrow."

"We need to get that policy clear as day, by the way."

She gives me a peculiar look. "Now who is Mr. Business?"

I place a croissant on her plate before setting one on my own. "I'm a lawyer. It's logical that I think of these things."

She gives up and sighs. "You perhaps have a point. Okay, it's just, while I'm here, I want you to continue your normal routine, and I will contribute where I can. I'm sure we both have our own schedules."

"We do. My days are long, which means we keep it to one round at night so I can have a good night's sleep."

Her laugh sounds good the way it bounces off the walls of my home. "Agreed… I'm really thankful. The moment this is too much then say the word, I can get out of your hair."

I don't bother looking at her as I butter my croissant. "It's all good." No, really.

"Well then…" Our eyes meet, and fresh air floats between us as we enter new territory together.

A few weeks ago, we were ready to throttle one another. Now? I can't get enough of her, and I'm convinced she feels the same. I didn't need to demand for her to stay yesterday, she was already on the cusp of gluing her feet to the floor.

Our soft, near giddy, smiles seem to stay permanent as we continue to eat our breakfast, and that feels too natural.

"What do you normally do on a Sunday?" I wonder.

"Often have a shoot, but by luck, the couple called Friday afternoon to reschedule." She speaks with her mouth full as it seems that she is famished.

An idea comes to me because all of my defenses to make her life miserable vanished and now I only want to do things to make her happy. "Want to head to Lake Spark for dinner at the Dizzy Duck Inn?"

Fondness appears on her face. "Ooh, that sounds good. But I noticed I need to go to the grocery store, as someone lives off of, well, protein bars and coffee? I'm surprised you had a roll of croissant dough and some bacon that is nearly at the expiration date."

Laughing to myself, I have to point out the obvious. "As much as I can say that it's the bachelor life, it's not. At work, we get meals since there is a chef for the players and most of the staff arrive early. Then often, I just BBQ with the guys or something."

"Makes sense. I would say you're welcome to come with me to the store, but that might be too tame for us."

"Actually, it's cool. I will tag along. No offense, but your coffee is only tolerable. We can grab a coffee from Foxy Rox."

"Deal. Oh, and I started a bunch of laundry to get the smell of smoke out from all of my clothes that were upstairs in my house. Hope you don't mind." Esme tucks a strand of hair behind her ear.

My lips quirk out, and I shake my head. "Not a problem. Want to head out soon?"

"Perfect."

Esme stands to take her plate away but seems to be stalled on her feet. "This is kind of weird, right? I mean, the way everything is transpiring?"

Licking my lips, I do all I can to suppress my smile, as I want to play it cool. "Apparently, the key was sourdough bread and a fire to scoot us along to something else."

"I guess so."

Our eyes linger for a good beat before the corners of her mouth jerk up, and she disappears into the kitchen.

My face collapses into my hands. What the fuck? Why are these feelings that I have for her unfolding so fast and rolling down a hill with nothing in the way to stop them?

Blowing out a breath, I push it all to the side and decide to just sway with the Sunday flow.

Esme and I sit across from one another at a small table outside Foxy Rox along the window, with coffee for me, tea for her, and a giant piece of peanut butter cake to share.

"See? The grocery store can be fun if you venture into

several aisles. Take your time to explore the objects on the shelf. You will now actually have all the basis of the food group pyramid in your house." Esme seems proud of herself.

I have to grin, as we have constantly joked with one another for the last two hours. The supermarket with her was purely hilarious. She debated which type of apples to buy, spent ten minutes in the cereal aisle, questioned if a tub of Greek yogurt should accompany the berries, and stocked the hell up on jars of pesto. When we reached the paper towels, then it was full-on like we were an old couple shopping together.

"You're right. I needed your wizard skills all along. I will no longer be a victim of choosing the wrong can of nuts or carton of milk."

She points her fork at me. "Oat milk is all the rage."

Stretching my arms over my head, I take in the fact that I haven't had a Sunday this laidback in a long time. "Sure. But your music tastes could be improved. Let's establish the whoever drives picks the music rule."

She scowls, but then it eases. "Fine."

My eyes lower to a table nearby where a giant dog with golden-brown fur is lying on the ground near a bowl of water that the café has for dogs. "Damn, he's gorgeous."

Esme glances over her shoulder to get a peek. "Wow, he is. I wish the fireman that came had a dog. Fire dogs are a thing, right? I was deprived a hot fireman and a cute dog, damn it."

I throw her the death stare. "Whoa there, cowgirl, you might want to take that back."

She smiles at me. "Only the fire dog part."

Quickly, I ask the couple what type of dog he is, and it's a golden retriever mixed with a Newfoundland dog. "I don't have time for a dog, but he would be a good contender if I did."

"Ah, so you are a dog person. Your soft soul is almost too sweet," Esme teases.

Shaking my head, I take the last sip of my coffee, but I don't want this all to end. "I think it's really good that you are not in complete misery after the fire."

Her smile slips away. "Well, I don't have much choice. In the end, I'm alive, right?"

The moment turns serious, but perhaps it should. "Still, you lost a kitchen, half of your living room, and pictures. It can't be easy."

She rolls a shoulder back. "My only option is to be optimistic. But it does hurt to have had this happen."

"That's a feeling you are allowed to have."

She sighs, and her eyes zip up to mine, not blinking once. "You were quite adamant that I didn't run in… Thank you."

I don't enjoy the constant thank-yous. "It was nothing. I'm sure you would have done the same for me."

"I guess I would have," she admits. Her fingers weave through her hair. "I'm sorry I was a pain in the ass the past few months."

The line of my mouth stretches. "I think I win the prize for being the resident jerk. The number of times I stormed across my yard by far outdoes your times."

Esme shrugs. "Flirtation does silly things to people. I wonder who won the neighborhood betting pool?"

I laugh under my breath. "Probably Oliver."

"I think so too." That unusual silence returns to us. "We are not labeling anything, are we? I mean, anyone could walk down Main Street right now and see that you and I are… together?" Her voice rises an octave.

I lean into the table and onto my arms. "That's not a

problem for me, is it for you?" No man gets to look at her the way I do. Nobody gets to think she needs a man and needs to be set up with someone. We might be in the oddest situation, but I was right the other week, and I don't share. I make claims.

"Not a problem for me, either." Her wide smile is do damn infectious; how can I not join her on that? She reaches across the table to touch my hand. "Want to head back to your place to drop the groceries off? I might have an idea."

My brow rises and my interest is piqued. "Oh yeah?"

She stands up and offers me her hand. "I'm going to go pay, and I'll meet you at the car."

"Not a chance. I'm a gentleman."

"And you're being kind by providing me a roof."

I yank her back when her feet move. "Trust me, my overtime billable hours for the Spinners mean I have money to spare on a thousand coffees."

Her eyes pop out. "Someone is conceited. But fine, I won't argue and will instead go wait in your expensive car that I only sometimes hate."

"Good."

She stands on her toes to give me a quick kiss.

I can't believe that I've been missing out on this, being tied down to someone. Or it's just Esme. But lucky me, I have her now.

―――

"Is this why you like wildflowers?" I ask as we walk along the clearing amongst the tall grass, making our way to a creek that I hear.

Esme has a wry smile as she leads the way. "Maybe. They are rustic and spontaneous. There is no logic to why they pop up where they are. Anything purple and white are my favorite."

"I don't believe that I've ever been out this way." It's picturesque.

She glances over her shoulder with a knowing look. "Because someone here struggles to stop and actually take a breath from work. Enjoy the quiet, will you?"

"Silence doesn't exist around you," I retort, but her smile brightens. "What is this place, exactly? Is this where you end my life and nobody can find the body?"

She grabs my wrist and leads as we arrive at the destination—an old pick-up truck with a stack of hay and overgrown grass close by and the creek in the background. I smile at the setting.

"It's where I do most of my photoshoots. There is a footbridge up there after the tree line, too. Even an old, broken-down water wheel on a mill." She indicates with her head. "It isn't private land, just not many people are aware of this place. At sunset, the light is amazing."

I circle in spot to truly examine the scene, and this is full-on prairie. Following her cue, I join her sitting on the back edge of the truck with our feet dangling.

"To be honest, as much as it is uplifting to take photos of couples heading toward forever, sometimes it's confronting."

"How so?"

She hums a sound. "I guess... life is good, except for my neighbor from hell." Esme bumps my arm with hers and smirks. "But life is just a movie. Fire aside, nothing is so wrong, and for many, they might think it's boring. Great friends, simple days. I haven't had much thought about the future, and maybe I should have. Lately, there have been little cracks that cause me to question life."

I adjust my body and lean back on my arms. "I can relate.

I haven't had much need to think past tomorrow in my personal life."

"Aren't we boring people."

"Nah, we're just like half of the adult population."

She lowers her sight to me, with her lips slanted to one side. "We should be the other half."

"Okay, then what do you see in your future?"

Esme thinks for a moment. "It's a blur except for flowers."

"I guess I need to get you another bouquet since my first effort was incinerated, just the way we used to be with one another."

"Used to be? Other than me now *temporarily* living with you, time will tell if our armistice will hold. I saw you leave a dish in the sink," she warns.

I laugh. "If that's the biggest concern, then we're doing okay."

She gently shoves me. "But seriously, I'm beginning to wonder if lack of direction is preventing me from something, I'm not sure what… maybe life-altering. I should use this house fire as that opportunity. Living situation, career, hobbies, the whole shebang."

I tap her arm with my own. "Then do it."

Esme snickers. "I guess. You know, when I found out that the house was left to me by my great-aunt, I wasn't sure I would move. First, I thought of renting it out, but then I thought of how I could have a little studio, and there is character in an old house. You have a house, but it's only a home if you make it that way. I'm going to miss it."

"You sound like it will never return," I say softly.

She shrugs. "Once everything is fixed, then maybe there won't be the same energy in the house."

"Is this the part where you inform me you feel the ghost

in your house will return or that we need to take a trip to that candle store that I told you about?"

She grins at me, appreciating my humor. "Tempting, but it's just… there is an overwhelming feeling that change is on the horizon. Surely, you've had a moment like that in life."

My jaw flexes side to side, doing my best to analyze my life. "In college, I had my eye on law school. Law school isn't always a breeze, but then you have your sight on your career. Once you establish your career, then you are too wrapped up in the workload to think beyond anything else. When I was hired for the Spinners, then that was career success mixed with a hobby."

"You played hockey… in high school," she deadpans.

The line of my mouth slants. "Fair point. But to further explain, there are only tiny moments where my mind is snapped out of my work grind."

Once I say it, I realize that nothing about this scenario seems appealing now that it's happened. Or rather, goals are checked off, so what now? Fuck, she has me thinking, and it's leading me down to my deeper subconscious.

She raises her brows. "Those tiny moments, such as?"

"Probably if I think to recently, then I think of my sister. First, my brother-in-law passing then my nephew entering the picture. Secondly, moving to Everhope and the renovations. But then… I got a hint of something else, something new and totally out of control." I encourage her to lean back and join me to lie down and stare at the blue sky with spotted white clouds.

"Everything of what you said is external. Someone else's life events, and I don't consider picking paint colors life-changing. Let me guess, you didn't even do that and had the designer handle that." My face strains, and her sidelong glance causes her to release a short laugh. "I knew it. Now tell me about this hint of something else. What is it?"

I pause for a second, wondering if I should really open this conversation, but I've never been a man to not be direct, it just doesn't normally involve feelings. "Well, I shouldn't be debating why negotiating with cocky sports agents have fallen low on my list, because it turns out there is someone I enjoy squaring off with more… You."

Her head lolls in my direction with the corner of her mouth tugging into a smile. "I think I might like that answer, even understand it."

"Good, because we might be arguing on the way home that you've taken me to a place where I'm confident I need to get a tetanus shot after."

Her eyes give me a fake glare before she inches closer to me.

"This sort of feels like being in high school and sneaking away with a guy to make out somewhere."

"Whoa, that took a turn in the conversation. I don't particularly care to hear about your younger self's escapades. Because I sure as hell… most definitely did the same."

We both chuckle and enjoy a moment of quiet, hearing only the birds chirping.

"Let's agree that we will both stop and evaluate our lives more to ensure we don't remain boring people with no route to a future dream." Esme offers her hand for me to shake.

My fingers touch her palm, and after a few seconds, I shake her hand. "Agreed."

"Phew, heavy conversation out of the way. You might still have a hot mess of a woman staying in your house once the adrenaline kicks off and the builders inform me that my house is as good as burnt toast, but at least I was optimistic for a few hours."

"Just shut your mouth, Esme, and let me make out with you."

She rolls on top of me. "If we must, Keats." She feigns the inconvenience.

It's one kiss, but then she stops, with so much beauty and fragility on her face. "Thanks for coming here. I've never actually been here with someone outside of photography. Just maybe… I'm happy it's you."

She doesn't let me process because she slams her mouth onto mine.

This is my life on pause. Seriously, stopping to smell the flowers, and it doesn't feel half bad; in fact, it feels downright positive and hopeful. There is something about this woman that has me spinning, and it appears I might just land in the right spot.

17

KEATS

Arriving down the stairs after showering after the gym, I find Esme towering over the kitchen island. I know this look. She isn't pleased, but my dick sure as hell is. The last few days it's been an admin nightmare with figuring out how to process the fire.

"You have some nerve."

My eyes grow wide. "Clue me in."

She folds her arms over her chest. "You hired a contractor without me!"

A smug smirk spreads on my mouth. "I did." And I don't regret it.

She begins to fume. "You can't just do that. It's *my* house that's burnt to a crisp."

I approach her with an easy stride, still feeling satisfied with my actions. "Yes, and after the adjusters come from both insurance companies, then things will need to move. Contractors are booked out long in advance, and Steven is a great one. He helped with my home."

Esme gawks at me. "I'm fairly confident that I can pick who is rebuilding."

I swing my finger up and wave it side to side as I tsk. "It's done, and it is one less thing that you need to worry about. Did you really want to interview potentials?"

Her mouth opens then closes. "I mean… I-I… well, okay, I have no clue what I'm doing, but that doesn't mean that you need to take control of the situation."

"Sure." I touch her cheek with my hooked finger before continuing my journey to the fridge. "Wine?"

Her mouth gapes open again. "Are you kidding me? What planet are you from where this is okay?"

"Planet earth." I open the door and search for that bottle of white we opened the other night.

"Maybe I hate *Steven's* process or he is too expensive or he simply pisses me off as much as Keats," she mocks.

Briskly closing the fridge door, I walk casually to the cupboard for two glasses. "Esme, you don't have much choice. His costs align with what you will probably get from the insurance payout, and he's making room in his schedule. Do you have any idea how many rich guys in this county want their houses renovated before the Arctic winter?"

She grumbles a sound but accepts the wine glass that I slide down the counter for her to drink. Esme drinks or rather gulps down a sip. "You might have a point, but still." One more growl for good measure, and damn it, I hate how adorable has become one of my top words lately.

But I sure as hell hope she doesn't figure out why I've made this gesture. Or maybe I do, ah hell, why not.

"I've made this easier for you, okay?"

She blinks a few times. "I just don't understand why you would take time to do this. It's like I need to be handheld and taken car—" She freezes mid-sentence as it dawns on her. "Taken care of," she rasps to herself.

Bingo. It's all I want to do, lately.

"Something like that," I state before enjoying my dry white.

She begins to step in my direction. "I mean, I guess I didn't want to search for builders… nor negotiate pricing." She rolls her shoulder back as if she doesn't want to make a big deal. She stares me down. "Or even try to understand what an adjuster does or how much I'll be getting." Her eyes soar up to me.

"Hmm. Imagine that. I'm not the bad guy." I clink our wine glasses in accomplishment.

"Doesn't mean you couldn't inform me beforehand."

"Meh, you would have disagreed, and then I would have had to throw you over my shoulder after our bitter argument."

At last, a half-smile cracks on her mouth. "You're probably right."

She stares at me and suddenly it's with admiration. "Thank you… I'm not used to someone taking care of me, and when my temper clears, then I can't help denying that, well… I like it a lot."

I shrug it off.

We observe one another, and the air shifts to calm, affectionate, and it seems she may float away happy.

But Esme sets her wine down and then removes my own glass from my hand. "Come on, Man Who Needs to Control Situations."

And she pulls me away before I can say a word.

My guestroom?

Huh.

Esme has mischief in her eyes as she hands me her camera and shows me the button to snap photos.

"Now turn around," she instructs. "And don't steal a glance."

"I'm only going along with this because the hockey season is over and there are no games to watch on TV." My eyes land on the floor where I notice her clothes are finding a new home.

"You may look."

Turning slowly around, I find Esme at the edge of the bed with a sheet not exactly wrapped around her, rather draped. Most of her legs can be seen and are in a provocative placement with one leg thrown over the other, exposing just enough of her ass that it's a tease. The sheet comes up between her legs, and she holds it barely around her breast. It's clear not a thread of sheet is covering her naked back. She's a sultry goddess with her hair down.

"What in the world are we doing?"

She crooks her finger and gestures me closer. "You can be the photographer for my boudoir shoot. The kind of photos that you hate to admit you love yet tease me about."

I smile tightly because I enjoy where her mind is at. "I'm on board with this."

Esme begins to crawl back, dragging the sheet with her in the sexiest way possible. "Then let's get started." Slowly, I approach the bed, not entirely sure what to do, and she notices. "Just take any photo you want. However, in this little session of ours, you will absolutely not see everything. A lot of skin, yes. Sacred parts, no." She lies back, and the sheet lowers slightly until her nipples can barely be seen.

"I believe I'm already enjoying this idea of yours." My knee dips into the mattress, and I shoot a photo from above as this beautiful woman is splayed across the bed. "Why in here?"

She rolls slightly to her side, creating an S shape with the sheet, her back and legs bare and just enough covering the front. "Better light. Perhaps, it also heightens the occasion, too. It might feel too ordinary in the bed that I seem to be sharing with you now."

Fuck, I'm getting hard. Esme puts effort into her different facial expressions that are new to me, yet it appears natural all the same. Her body moves tantalizing slow after I take photos in certain positions.

"How in the world do you do this and not, well..."

Her head falls back in laughter, displaying her elongated neck in the process. "It's a job, and the many reasons that women do this remind me that it's important to give them photos they will cherish. Besides, I think it's different when you do this with someone you are very familiar with..."

My head retreats back in concern. "You've done this before?"

Her big toe points into the mattress, giving me another view that's too enticing, but I'll stay professional for her. "No," Esme answers bluntly. "You're the first who gets to take photos of me like this."

I pause for a second to examine her and the sincerity in her eyes. "Lucky me then." Very.

She rises on her knees to come face to face with me, with the sheet fisted near the middle of her breasts. "I have a confession," she rasps before she gently with purpose removes the camera from my hands and sets it on the mattress next to us. Her eyes return to me with strong conviction.

"What might that be?" I whisper, completely mesmerized by her beauty.

Esme begins to dust my lips with her own, a mere brush but nothing more. "The mail..."

"What about it?" I chase her mouth, attempting to trap her

lips. "Is this about the fact that even the mailman looking at you pisses me off?"

She wobbles once and lets go of the sheet, but it stays put as our bodies are wound together tightly. "I wrote the wrong address."

"And?" I do my best to capture her lips.

"On purpose." I feather my hands up her bare back until I cup her face. "Already two months ago, I did it." Her breath is heavy. "More than once."

The corner of my mouth curls. "I was hoping you were doing that," I admit softly. "Then and now."

There is a vulnerable gleam in her eyes when we look at one another, but it's only a few seconds before I crash my lips down onto hers.

I'm relieved and happy that it appears this relationship between us isn't one-sided.

18

ESME

Clicking on my computer screen, I'm struggling to focus. Probably because it's 5:30 in the morning and the sun is only starting to appear in the sky. I sit on the sofa in the living room and a smile pulls on my mouth.

There is something about waking to find Keats lying next to me. Even when sleeping, he appears serious, or rather, I haven't seen any smiles slip through when he's dreaming. It's doable though, as I'm lucky that his arm tends to venture my way to keep me cuddled against him.

Sometimes I used to wake early because the focus was there, but lately, it's because my house next door is in a crisis. It's one giant mess with the insurance companies and ordering things for the contractor. It's a different ball game when you have to build after a fire. It's a lot of waiting time. Even when Keats walked through the house with the inspector, his sharklike legal mentality didn't get me far.

But it's okay. As much as my house is my home, I'm enjoying the temporary stay at my neighbor's. In fact, in a warped way, I feel lucky. It might have only been two weeks, but every day something inside of me blooms open.

This man has me twisted.

In a knot.

One that I don't want to be undone.

I'm lost in this living dream, which is why I don't hear Keats walk down the stairs, already in his work clothes.

"You're up before me. Now who needs the workaholic talk?" He walks behind the couch and leans down to kiss my lips. Morning kisses are his softer side.

"Mmm, good morning to you too," I greet him.

Keats continues his journey to the kitchen, and I close my laptop to follow. In the kitchen he turns on his coffee machine while he yawns and stretches.

"You shouldn't work on the couch like that. It will kill your wrists."

I choke a laugh. "I'm going to yoga in a little bit. Besides, you work at your coffee table when you are bored with your dining table, even though you have an office in this little mansion of yours. Someone is hypocritical." Coyly, I smile. "Your concern is more that my wrist action and hands would be out of service."

His tongue swipes across his front teeth. "Not even six a.m. and your very dirty mind is out in full force."

Pattering to his waiting arms, he kisses the top of my head. "Look at us starting our day with a tiff," I joke.

"Yeah, yeah, yeah. Now time to grab my bran flakes and milk," he says, not exactly enthused, but I've forced him to add breakfast to his morning routine. I know he gets stuff at the office, although it's off season, so the breakfast options are smaller than during regular game season since not many people are there. Sometimes I feel like this desire to take care of him is a built-in instinct of mine. Doesn't matter. What is important is that I *want* to do these things for him.

"Breakfast of champions for my hardworking thirty-three year old man," I tease, and I wrap my arms around his middle with no intention of leaving because breakfast can wait a few minutes.

I notice the way he inhales the scent of my shampoo, "white rice lily" it's called.

Maybe we are overly cute together. Is it because we're new? I don't question it anymore. We go at our own pace, and it just so happens to be from freezing to boiling in what many would consider a short time. We're not definable, but we stir emotions in the other even if we don't discuss it.

"What's on your agenda today?"

"Catching up with Hailey this morning after yoga. That reminds me, you wanted to do a BBQ this weekend, right?"

Keats steps away to actually grab his breakfast materials because he listens to me. "Why not? The weather is supposed to be great. You only have a shoot early afternoon. My sister wants to come over, and it's always fun to watch the Liam, Hailey, and Oliver show."

I chuckle because he is right. Little nerves flutter up inside of me. "Your sister," I state.

His back is to me when he closes the fridge door with milk in hand, but I can see the corner of his face that has an amusing smirk. "Freaking out much? I thought you two hit it off."

I snort a laugh. "Back when I thought you were insufferable."

Keats opens the cereal box. "Ooh, Esme is shaking in her boots."

Raising one foot, grateful that I'm flexible, I show him my bare toes. "No socks or shoes on."

"Relax. Besides, my nephew is the distraction."

I am slightly eased. "Well, just let me know what to get at the grocery store."

"Will do. I'll be home late tonight. Work and all."

I'm used to it. Sometimes he is home around dinner, and we eat something casual and catch up, but there are many days he gets home when I'm asleep since I hit a 9 p.m. nosedive on the tired scale. It's understandable why it must be difficult to sustain a relationship which is why he's been single for a while, but we puzzle together. Schedules don't seem to bother us; we respect the lines.

"I'll be sleeping."

He points his spoon at me. "You won't be five minutes after I get home." He winks. Sometimes in my drowsy state we end the day on a positive naked note, other times right before the alarm goes off in the morning.

Despite our living arrangement, domesticated us hasn't worn down the passionate us.

"Just go. You're going to be late." I shoo him.

He takes another bite of his cereal that he never finishes and listens to me and gathers his stuff.

After he grabs his laptop bag that was sitting on the counter, he stops by me for a kiss. "Go back to bed. You barely slept, and there is nothing you can do about your house right now."

My lips press together, listening but not believing.

Keats's affection is only soft and sweet for a few moments before he playfully slaps my ass as he moves on. "It's an order that you need to follow, otherwise later there will be consequences."

He isn't even joking.

Nor am I when internally I want the words to roll off my

tongue that I'm not worried about my house because I only think about him.

Hailey pours wine into my tumbler as we stand in the kitchen, preparing a snack plate for everyone outside.

"You and Keats," she says in a melody.

I give her the death stare. "Here we go."

She grins and sips on her white. "What? Am I crazy for asking? It's like night and day. Before you two hid your attraction behind a mask of fury, and now, you don't hide a single thing. In fact, I would say you've long moved on from just flirtation."

Popping a cube of cheese into my mouth, I ponder for a few seconds. "We have," I agree. "In our own blurred lines kind of way."

Hailey throws her hands together and squeezes them near her heart with a beaming smile. "Happy to hear. You two look good together. His eyes move so possessively over you, and you can tell how much he cares for you. It must be great to have a guy who knows what he wants."

My face puzzles. "You're talking about me, right?"

She looks flustered. "Totally," she squeaks.

I place my wine glass down with aggravation. "Screw the brother's-best-friend rule and just go at it like rabbits already, okay?"

Hailey shakes her head in frustration. "It's not that easy. Besides, Mr. Hotshot Lawyer can make a move, but he doesn't, which means he is a coward. I deserve better."

"Keep saying that to yourself and maybe one day you will be convinced."

She throws a cracker at me. "No diversion. Back to you

and the guy you are living with. This isn't like one of those living together getting close situations, and then poof there are feelings, is it?"

Glancing outside the window by the sink, my eyes catch with Keats's, and he holds his beer bottle up with a soft smile.

"What if I said I think it's more? Or rather, I have an uncontrollable feeling that maybe a life that you share with someone can all come true?"

Hailey smiles brightly at me. "Lucky you then. You're getting something you deserve. My friend is in a relationship that is heading somewhere."

My mouth opens to protest, but the words get stuck because it would be a lie. "I think so, too," I confidently agree. Still, I don't want to jinx myself because we're still unconventionally living together, this isn't a permanent arrangement, and maybe the novelty will wear off. But in the pit of my stomach, I don't believe it will, nor do I want it to fade.

Never in a million years would it have crossed my mind that I would end up in this very spot with feelings new to me. They're consuming me, too.

We're having fun but are not afraid to confront each other about aspects of our life.

Damn it, why did I wait so long to give in to him?

The squeal of a child draws our attention outside, and my insides turn into a puddle.

Summer and Bo have just arrived. Keats's nephew wobbles his way, clearly excited to see his uncle who is leaning down to his level with open arms. Summer trails behind carrying a grocery bag since Bo has only one destination in mind. Keats hugs his nephew then picks him up. Watching him is an image, the way he holds his nephew on one hip when he stands, holding his beer bottle in his other hand. It's not for the faint of heart, either.

"Damn, you're drooling." Hailey giggles.

I glance seriously to her. "Do you not see what I see?" I gesture outside where Summer leaves her son in good hands and heads our way to drop off the bag.

"Oh, I do, but it's my friend seeing a flicker of a longer timeline. A preview, if you will."

Glowering, I warn her. "Stop it. Can we focus on the now, please? Did you not get the memo that we are not 100% sure what we are?"

She isn't listening. "No, because I'm the one watching the show and seeing the obvious. Now, if you'll excuse me, I need to remind the guys that a well-done burger makes me happy."

She grabs her wine glass and strides away through the French doors to the back patio. As she leaves, Summer walks in, and I gulp.

"Hey there." She smiles and sets her grocery bag on the counter.

"Hi."

Summer tries to conceal her ear-to-ear grin, but she really can't. "Enjoying my brother's hotel?"

"I…" I also can't seem to hide my smile. "It's fine."

She inspects me in a curious way. "I think it's great that he isn't alone. I'm sure you are keeping him in line, too."

Shrugging, I decide to focus on the snack plate that I gave up on. "Maybe." I feel her eyes on me and perhaps she's having a field day with this whole situation.

"I'm sorry about your house. Well… This might sound vicious but also not, it brought you closer to my brother."

My eyes flick up in surprise. "You barely know me."

Summer slides up onto the kitchen counter and begins to

unpack the bag. "I don't need to. Just hearing my brother talk about you and seeing his smile now is enough."

My heart feels light due to her observation, and my body straightens from the boost of assurance. "I'm not sure what to say."

"Nothing. Sometimes we don't need to use many words." She pulls out a box of animal crackers.

"Oh, Keats mentioned Bo likes those, and I already got a box at the store. I think it's in the pantry."

She is struggling to contain her smile, and I can tell that she's thinking to herself. "I think that he might be a family man, even if he hasn't figured it out. Or maybe it's not for him."

"I think he just wants to be a great uncle."

She shakes her head. "I think he just realized that he can have someone in his life. Because I'm nosy and ask wildly rude questions when it is none of my business, do you want a husband and kids one day?"

My eyes grow bold, as Keats's sister isn't afraid. "Uh, wow, you're really going for it. I haven't really thought about it until now."

Summer claps her hands together. "Perfect. You two are on the same timeline and just working at your own pace toward what you two want, and I don't just mean kids, I mean the whole future outlook."

I choke a laugh. "You sound very convinced."

Her shoulders slant up to her ears. "It could be that I'm excited because I haven't seen my brother this way, but it's more because he needs someone on his level. He's always been headstrong."

"Oh, I know," I agree.

"It also means that he needs a sort of partner. Enter you."

"Hmm. Well, this is kind of strange for you to be so… enthusiastic."

She laughs. "Esme, my brother talked about you long before you two got together. Surely, you know that. His pretend complaints were so apparent."

I bite my inner cheek because it makes me content to hear because our behavior goes both ways. "I see." I play it cool.

"Anyhow, it's awesome. I'm happy. He's happy, and it's all good."

I appreciate her effort to ease me. I'm not sure what I was expecting today. Lifting the snack plate, I feel safe enough to close the conversation and move on to a relaxing dinner, but as I move, my feet remain cemented to the kitchen floor.

Taking a deep breath, I go for it. "I care about him."

Summer studies me with appreciation. "Good. He really is a great guy, and once he gets something he wants, then he tends to never let it go." Her eyes are tense when they meet mine, but they still keep that light inside me burning.

The sound of the door opening breaks our conversation.

"Is my sister being a pain in the ass?"

She gawks at him. "Shall we replay the last year and your sound advice?" Summer pats his shoulder in passing. "I'm repaying in full."

We both watch her leave, and if I'm honest, I envy their family dynamic. Keats turns to me with his hands in his pockets. "Everything alright?"

"More than." I peer down to the snack plate. "This is literally the slowest creation of veggies, cheese, crackers, and hummus. I've made you all starve while we wait for the burgers."

Keats chuckles and waits for me as I circle around the island and stop in front of him. He brings his lips to mine to steal a kiss. "You're forgiven. Just wanted to check that you are still alive and Summer hasn't shared any embarrassing stories about my high school hockey days."

I flash my eyes at him. "I shall never say."

I walk away, but I can't help noticing that he dawdles behind to observe me, and one quick view over my shoulder informs me that he's pleased that I'm here.

Every minute lately keeps tightening that knot between us.

And there are no complaints.

19
KEATS

Damn. Family-and-friends BBQ now has a new meaning.

I was able to tear my eyes away after seeing a few seconds of Esme chatting with the women while playing catch with my nephew which entails a gentle toss while he stands next to her. Then there is the fact that my sister keeps winking at me in approval which is now exhausting.

But still, it all just feels comfortable.

"Yeah, a Colorado wedding next summer," Liam informs us while he scoops up the last burger on the grill with the spatula.

"Destination wedding here we come," Oliver says.

"Just let us know the date to see if I can pencil you into my calendar," I add.

The guys chuckle. "Grouchy workaholic, here we come," Liam notes.

Oliver nudges my shoulder. "Nah, he's toned it down a bit since he has a woman living with him."

"What's the deal with that, by the way? Esme just moves

on out when her house is repaired? That's like taking a step back in your relationship," Liam makes his thoughts known.

"Well, it is her home. It's not like it's just going to be an empty house once it's fixed," I note, and it kind of stings that it's the logistics, because I'm beginning to feel that she belongs somewhere else.

Oliver looks at me strangely. "I heard her mention that it will take at least three months to be fixed. That's quite a timeframe to live together. Surely, you get attached and stuff."

I shrug. "Haven't really thought that far. We're just, you know, going with it. Day by day."

The guys look between one another then focus their attention on me. "Hmm, okay." Oliver speaks on their behalf with the most unconvinced tone.

"What else am I supposed to say?"

"I mean, I guess nothing," Liam admits.

Oliver just continues to have his cheeky smirk. "When you start to see past day by day, then it's your sign, buddy."

I gawk at him for a hot second. "Oh really?" I deadpan, and that causes his demeanor to recoil.

My sister arrives to our circle with a grin, and she crosses her arms. "I'm liking what I see, big brother." She looks around the guys, and they are all teaming up on me.

"Let's just hope he doesn't screw it up," Liam mentions.

"Geez, you are all ferocious tonight." Perhaps a little too honest for us all. I'm not entirely sure what it is that I could do right now to turn my current life into a disaster, but I'm not immune to the fact that I'm not perfect. Maybe lately has been too good to be true. Fear isn't something that I experience often, but why is it dripping somewhere inside of me?

Liam closes the BBQ lid and then diverts his attention back to me. "I'm not saying you need to lock it in right now. It's still early days. I think we just mean that this whole being with someone, and a normal human compared to past options, is new for you. No need to run away if things get tough."

"We keep talking as though they are a sure thing, but it's still early for them," Oliver reminds us all.

My sister waves them off. "Doesn't matter."

"Oh, look at that, dessert time." I pivot sharply to escape, and I hear them chuckling in the background.

I still have a grin on my face because they all mean well. That doesn't mean they haven't succeeded at stirring things inside my head.

I'm not a fan of the unknown. Laws are set, paperwork has deadlines, it's either a yay or nay when negotiating. Not much room for the undetermined.

Which is why in my non-work life I'm going around in circles.

It's only scaring me in tiny increments.

THE REST of the evening was simple. Smooth conversations, a slow dinner, and my usual reminder to my sister that she can crash here and Bo can sleep in the portable crib. Normally, she takes me up on the offer, but she just laughed me off and said she was going home so I could have alone time with Esme. I had to take a moment to remind myself that I'm still on planet earth, as this is a whole new scenario for me.

But here I am sliding into bed after a shower. Esme took hers when I was cleaning the grill.

Her tiny satin shorts and matching tank are frustrating. Perfectly hot on her, but it just means more fabric to get off.

"I had fun," she informs me.

"Yeah, simple but nice."

She chortles a laugh before she rolls to her side. "Anything but simple. I got the third degree from just about everyone."

A droll smile hangs on my mouth. "You too, huh?"

"It was... confronting?" She grimaces.

I laugh out loud. "Something like that." My cheeks hurt from how much smiling I've done today. "Hey, I was thinking that you should make your own desk area, that whole sanctuary thing. I have my spare room that is supposed to be an office, but I don't use it," I suggest since she's been using her laptop in corners of my house.

She swats me. "I'm here temporarily, remember? Setting up a desk feels a little... like a big step." She seems unsure of her words.

I look at her strangely, internally not liking her words either. "Penny for your thoughts?" My voice is uneven.

She grins, as we are both tiptoeing around the bluntness that we normally have. "I'm just thinking about our pace. The speed of our relationship developing," she answers for us. "I like this little world you and I have created and found ourselves in."

Her eyes sparkle differently. Promising. But they're searching for an answer from me.

"We're on the same page." A silence stretches between us. "Hey, Esme."

Her lips pinch together as she waits patiently for me to finish my thought.

"Sometimes you watch me sleep. I wake and you're there. I know I'm great to look at." I sound a little conceited, but it's to lighten the mood. "But I never know if you'll be there or not as the first thing I see in the morning." Damn, do I sound near vulnerable?

She smirks to herself. "That's good, as every day shouldn't be the same."

A warm smile syncs with a feeling for her that claws inside of me.

Still, I might have a different kind of statement to make. I reach into the bedside table drawer and pull out the handcuffs. This isn't our first time bringing these out.

"Hands up above your head," I demand with swelter in my voice.

Instantly, the demeanor changes between us, with Esme's mouth parting and a sultry look gracing her face.

All smiles are gone because I like taking command of her body with a firm understanding that I'm taking the lead. I clasp the cuffs around her wrists through the slats of the headboard, and I lie on my side with my eyes exploring her body. Bringing my finger up, I gently outline the bottom of her flimsy top that lifts to just above her belly button. The simple act causes her nipples to turn into little pebbles.

"We may be on an unclear path…" I rasp then watch my fingers walk down under her waistband but stopping, her body writhing from the touch. "But you're mine. Is that clear?"

"Yes," Esme husks.

I dive down and use my teeth to tug on the fabric over her breasts, grazing just enough to make her shiver.

Covering her nipple with my warm breath, I circle my tongue, with the satin acting as a wall. Her breath turns heavy, and her body lifts up into my touch. I begin to kiss her body and slither down. My fingers slip into her little boxers to touch her heat.

"This is all for me, isn't it?" I stroke her pussy, my fingers already soaked.

"Only for you," she breathes heavily.

I adjust until I'm lying on my stomach next to her, halfway down her body, and I lift her camisole high until her breasts are on display. I drag my lips below her belly button while I circle her clit with the pad of my finger. "Such a needy girl." My tongue darts out and firmly draws a line down to her boxers that I'm using my free hand to lower. But I stop right where she doesn't want. "Beg, Esme."

"Please. Keats, please. You can take whatever you want. I'm all yours," she keens.

Rewarding her, my tongue finds her swollen click to flick, and her moan is instant. She does her best to press against my mouth, but I hold her hips down. My face is almost upside down as I lick her. The woman I share a bed with and who is willing to push limits when we want to.

"Open your thighs nice and wide."

Her knees butterfly out, and I caress her inner thigh up and down. "Good girl," I murmur against her clit.

"Keats," she grits out. "Please."

My head shoots up to look at her face. "Behave, Esme. Or I'll flip you to your stomach, spank you, and take you from behind while I yank your hair," I warn her.

She licks her lips, enjoying the idea. Silly me, that's exactly she wants, and lucky for her, I want to give what she desires.

I chuckle deeply in warning. "Roll over, my eager little demon."

We work together until she is on her stomach, and I give her one good spank, and she yelps but then lifts her ass because she wants to be on offer. Positioning myself, I lift her hips a little higher, and I lean over to wrap her hair around my hand, tugging with her breath a near pant.

"Don't say that I didn't warn you."

"Keats, I'm begging. Please."

I skim around her opening. "Why would I listen and give in so easily?"

She shoots me a coy smirk over her shoulder. "Because I'm yours."

"Such a good girl."

I reward her and push in, our moans blending until I'm in as deep as I can go. I don't go easy. I slam into her repeatedly, intent on making her whimper and moan. Every thrust always hitting that spot and filling her to the hilt, while her body jiggles from my blunt force.

By the time we're coming, we're both screaming from an orgasm due to her pussy vibrating around my cock and my release feeling like I've jumped off a cliff.

The moment we both seem to calm our breath, I begin to place soft kisses up her spine until her neck, and gently, I let go of her hair. Slipping out of Esme, she drops her hips and twists to her back with a droll smile and her face flushed.

Returning to my side, I ensure our eyes meet before I feather over her lips, placing a kiss. Reaching up, I unlock the cuffs, and she shakes her arms back down. I steal another kiss, my thumb circling her cheek.

Barely parting, her tongue glides along my bottom lip. "Yours," she whispers.

"Only mine."

My hand skirts along her curves, soothing her body that I was perhaps a little rough with.

"You okay?" I check.

She giggles and falls forward, with her forehead touching mine. "More than."

Landing on my back, I take her with me until she is wrapped across my body.

"You always do this to me." Her voice is drowsy. "Not letting me leave the bed, which means you're dripping down my thighs." I can hear the smile in her voice.

Kissing the top of her head, I rub my palm in circles on

her back. "Marking you the way I like it." It's an overpowering ownership that must be some caveman mentality.

"Maybe I like it, too. But next time will you blindfold me?" she requests with not an ounce of sarcasm because she's serious.

That's my girl.

A funny thing about blindfolds. They might prevent you from seeing.

But they make you feel more.

20

ESME

Clasping the clip in my hair, I growl as the contractor explains the timeline ahead.

"Are you sure?" I double-check as we stand in my living room that has now been cleared and is ready for renovation.

Steve, the man in his thirties, stares at me with pain in his expression and a pencil behind his ear. "We keep running into more issues. We need to rebuild the wall and redo the floors, and it's best to do that in every room downstairs. Redoing the electrical won't be easy, as this is an older home, and we have to start from scratch due to the fire. Not to mention, it will take at least six to twelve weeks for your kitchen cupboards to arrive once ordered. Then there is the fact that we also have drywall to hang, and the cement on the ground floor needs to set."

I gave up on listening to his list when he mentioned twelve weeks. "So, when you add all of that together?" I'm afraid to ask.

His head falls as he checks his thoughts. "For sure six

months. I know your insurance will cover everything, but that can't speed up infrastructure."

My palm flies up to stop him. "I'm aware," I say sadly.

"You have it better than your neighbor. Their contractor is a friend, and he said they are basically going to fix up the basics and resell. It's too much work for them."

Pinching the bridge of my nose, I remind myself to count my blessings. "Mrs. Tiller is going to live with her daughter. As spunky as that old woman is, this could probably have all been avoided if she, well, maybe… It doesn't matter. Here I am with a boarded-up wall."

He humors me and takes a few steps to place his moisture measurement tool against the one wall still intact; he already told me his findings but maybe he feels the need to confirm again. "I'm sorry, Esme. There is also damage from when the fire department put out the fire. A lot of moisture that needs to be cleared."

Rubbing my face, I remember that my expectations were aligned with this conversation, but it still hurts to actually be confronted with it. Following Steve to the front door, there is nothing more to say. "Well, thank you again. I guess… go ahead and fix everything further that surprises us. We don't have much other choice."

We walk out into the sun, and I close the door behind me. Stopping near his truck, we finish up our conversation.

"We'll get on it next week since we need to adjust our schedule. My crew is finishing up a job in the next few days. Normally, we are booked up, but I would rather take on this big project than a bunch of little projects."

I attempt to smile in appreciation, but the corners of my mouth only manage a tiny tilt. "Thanks for that. I'll make sure there is coffee and donuts."

"Much appreciated, but it's going to be a long few

months, so don't you run up a donut bill from Foxy Rox," he jokes.

"Sure thing." Steve opens his car door, but as he is about to close it, a thought comes to me. "Hey… do you think that next week I can take the hammer to either nail something in or destroy something, anything to get out some frustration?"

It causes him to stifle a laugh. "Deal. You take care now."

"Thanks."

I sigh as he drives away and mope myself over to the street to check the mailboxes just as Keats rolls up in his car with his window down. He's home early.

"Did I get some of your mail again?" he says in jest.

My attempt to laugh is tempered by this afternoon's news. "Looks like you might be receiving my mail for a long time to come."

Keats has a peculiar look. "I'll meet you inside."

I lift my nose as a reply then open both boxes to find that no mail has been delivered today.

With a lack of energy, I head back inside to Keats's house. Something else is bothering me right now, but I just can't pinpoint it.

Walking to the kitchen, Keats came in via the side door and he's already setting his laptop bag on a stool.

"You really should use that desk you have. That kitchen chair is basically a shelf," I comment for the thousandth time. My low energy is sometimes when my wit comes out in full.

He licks his lips, trying to hold back a retort because he senses my low energy.

"The desk is waiting for you, if you want it. But someone said that's as big a step as making me a pie. Now, what happened?" He leans against the counter with ankles crossed as he unbuttons his cufflinks. It's my daily dose of Keats's natural swagger that is distracting and fills my body with an uncontrollable hunger for this man.

Fluttering the lids of my eyes, I remind myself to stay focused. "My house issue is a lot bigger than we thought. The contractor and I walked through now that the debris has been cleared. My next step is to head to a kitchen store. I'm not even sure where to begin with all of this. Perhaps I'm overwhelmed." Or it's something else simmering under the surface.

"Hmm, well, did you really think it would all be solved faster?"

My head bows low. "No. It's just… you're being very kind for me to stay here, but this is going to be a lot longer than planned and maybe…" Is this what is bothering me?

Keats doesn't move; instead, he has a cunning look, the kind that can chain me down. "You think it's an issue?"

Rolling my eyes to the side, I hate that he has a key to my thoughts. "Perhaps."

"Hmm." He is making that sound again because he already has a theory in his head and he's sticking to it. "It's not an issue."

"It could be months," I recap what I learned today.

His facial expression remains poised. "And?"

My tongue glides along my upper lip, trying to think of a better angle to approach this since I have a sexy statue in my presence. "We're kind of jumping into the deep end, maybe? It's only been a few weeks, and we now face the prospect that I'm not leaving anytime soon."

Now his face eases, except into a smirk which is just as damaging. "It's more than a month or two that we've been going back and forth, getting to know one another through spirited debate before we transpired with broken pearls on my hallway floor."

Walking a delicate line, I approach him because everything is emerging from a cloud. "You're very right, but still, it's a step, and then when my house is ready, I move back." Is this me testing him?

Keats seems taken aback. "Oh... yeah... right. Makes sense. You have a house, after all." Is that disappointment I hear?

Then it dawns on me, that whisper inside me that wasn't clear. What it is that has me uneasy. The realization of the true reason I've been miserable today.

Because one day my house will be ready for me again.

Which means I won't be here.

Because I'm beginning to realize that my old simple life, where I was going through the motions day to day, now feels different. There is someone who causes me suddenly to see everything in a different light. It's excitement and wanting to be there for them.

I'm not the greatest at showing that, we've kind of only been together on the surface. We've avoided confronting what lies deep within.

"Silly, huh?" I attempt to laugh, but it's nimble and lacking honesty. I step closer to the man that is as good as a boyfriend if we are really going to call it like it is. My hands find a place on either side of his body, resting on the counter. He loops his arms around me to yank me close so our middles touch.

"I mean, we'll be neighbors who share a bed sometimes," I clarify, and the thought sounds like misery. I'm tiptoeing my words to build to what we really are.

More.

I want to be the same to him as the way he treats me.

Important to one another. Caring. Exhilarating each other.

"Neighbors." His jaw ticks. "I guess that's the case," he

replies, his tone neutral. It doesn't help me in my attempt to assess where his mind is at.

Swallowing, I feel as though I put a damper on the mood. Keats arrived home early which means we can have dinner and open a bottle of wine. He will soon be away on a business trip for almost a week. But right now, neither one of us seem to be hungry.

"I have a house, after all," I'm nearly mute when I remind us both.

I'm beginning to want to scream desperately that I always want to stay here, house be damned.

But I'm afraid to say it.

Being hurt by someone who you lo— is new to me.

Keats gives me a tender kiss on my forehead before firmly setting his fingers on my shoulders. "Of course... I'm going to check up on some emails then pack."

He's avoiding me. He never packs so far in advance. He isn't leaving for a few days.

"Sure," I reply simply, but I'm disappointed inside.

I forgot to calculate another aspect of our dynamic.

Before we used to go in circles through sniping and glares at each other. Now we're in uncharted territory of communicating without a fight.

Our game was always who could bark the loudest. Now it's who dares to speak the truth first.

And I'm not sure it's me.

Hailey points to another tile on the wall as we peruse the store.

"Nah, I'm not a fan of the navy blue. The backsplash should be sleek and glossy white," I say.

It feels like hours as we explore the possibilities for my new home.

A home that is fading away to being simply called a house.

Her finger falls, and she quickly coughs into her arm. "Esme, six months ago you would have shown up here with a mood board. Today you look like a freaking ghost."

We continue to tread along the aisle. "I'm just tired. Keats is about to go away for work, and I think I've made it so everything feels kind of off. I'm positive it's because of the living situation."

"You're not being the ideal living partner? Getting annoyed with one another already?"

I shrug. "It's not that. It's more the murky waters we've found ourselves in, and I really need to clearly state what I want." Hailey sneezes again. "Geez, did you have to tag along with your disease?"

"Sorry," her response is nasally. "The worst is over. I was in bed with a temperature and stomach flu, then it stopped, but it's been replaced with this."

I throw her an unimpressed glare. "Thanks. Now you're spreading your germs to me."

"You'll be fine. You have the immune system of champions since you see clients all the time."

"I'm not on board with that logic, and I have a shoot to get through, so don't curse me." She chuckles at me since I'm being a little grouchy. "Anyhow, perhaps Keats going away for a few days is a good thing. A bit of breathing room. We've kind of been pedal to the metal and maybe haven't stopped to assess. We can't seem to slow down. And I need to prepare myself to be open with him."

I shake my head again when she points to another tile that is missing the glossy finish I want.

"I think you probably already know what it is you want long-term. It's just you literally have a house between you two. Empty houses can be confronting since it either needs to be sold or have someone living there. You two just decided to add a layer of complication, being in a relationship and neighbors. Surely, you can't be the first people to find themselves in this situation. Did you internet search this or something?" Her truth mixed with humor will keep me going this afternoon.

"Sure. I'm totally going to take advice from Jennifer in Ohio from my search results, who posted a message on some random message board," I answer.

Hailey grabs my arm to stop me. "Hot customer at twelve o'clock," she speaks in a hushed tone.

I step back due to her tenacity. "You only came with me to pick up guys?"

She laughs out loud. "Nah, but it never hurts to look at eye candy. He looks like a doctor our age who is remodeling his house. Perhaps has good taste, as he's surveying the subway tile." Hailey has a skill where she can sense everyone's backstory. Makes conversations interesting.

"Can we, uh, stay focused?"

Her sight returns to me with reverence in her eyes. "I am. You're two torrid lovers stuck at a crossroads to evaluate your relationship, even though it's blatantly obvious. For someone who is known to be ruthless in a suit, your gentleman suitor needs to step it up on the direct communication front and share his views on the relationship issue of where you two are heading next. Meanwhile, my dear friend is too petrified to be the first to jump in, but she knows what she wants and is preparing to tell him. Anything else I need to know?"

I have a wry smile due to her evaluation that is spot-on.

"Every time you talk to me, doesn't it feel as though I'm constantly assessing my situation?"

Hailey smirks to herself. "That's because you want only one thing and that's a future with him," she casually voices her views before pointing at another tile option.

A future.

That *is* what I see.

It makes me giddy and excited. Scared yet ecstatic. The logistics can be figured out later because my priority now is to make my feelings clear. Not just about where we are in a moment but where we are heading.

I've never been afraid of Keats before. He was always my sparring partner.

All the more reason I should avoid the idea that it's daunting to lay it all out and instead take the plunge.

I will admit everything.

Now I just hope he feels the same.

Keats leans over me upside down as I lie on the sofa. He kisses my forehead, and his palm glides down my cheek before he returns to standing.

"Go away," I growl. My entire body aches, my nose is stuffy, and my ability to think clearly is muffled by my headache.

"Someone is a little frosty today." He smirks.

I have no energy to protest. "I just don't want to get you sick." Hailey needs to be cursed for infecting me.

"You're going to be okay while I'm away?" He's already unfolding the throw blanket on the chair arm and splaying it on top of me before I can even answer.

I'm kind of frustrated that I've been under the weather

since last night. All ability to proclaim my feelings has kind of fallen off the table. Plus, Keats is occupied with his trip.

"I'll be fine. I'm just going to down some medicine like it's tequila and sleep," I assure him.

"I hope you feel better soon."

Me too.

I haven't forgotten the emotion inside of me that swirls like a hurricane ready to be unleashed, but I want the setting to be right and not when I have a killer headache and stuffy nose.

Propping myself onto my forearms, I watch as he winds up the cord to his phone charger to tuck into his laptop pocket. "When you get back maybe we can have an evening in and talk?" I ask.

He nearly drops the charger as his brows furrow. "Something I need to worry about?"

I smile because I realize my choice of words might send his thoughts into different directions. "No, I just thought a week apart is good for us. A chance to take a breath and not let our thoughts be jaded by our current situation." My eyes swim around the room. "As in me living under your roof and, of course, logistics, really."

Keats remains poised, but his eyes darken. "Right, we need to talk about that. I guess not letting you escape and tying you to a bed won't be a sustainable solution." His smile is weak, but that just means he's covering his true thoughts.

Still, I half laugh, and it turns into a cough, but when it clears, my smile returns. "Just a talk," I promise. *Except to tell you I really feel for you. An uncontrollable outpouring of contentment to be with you, full-on. I'm beginning to believe that L-word is only meant for you.*

"I guess you're right, about the whole space thing," he speaks.

Oh, maybe I just shot myself in the foot and life isn't so promising.

Except Keats parades back to me, and I'm melting. "Distance does things to people. Knowing you and me, it will lead us down an unusual path." The man actually swoops up my hand to kiss. What a chaste and saccharine gesture.

"You're really being annoying." I grin.

"Oh, but you love it." He pecks my lips quickly before he saunters away to his luggage in the entryway to the living room. "If there is anything then just call," he reminds me and gently knocks on the frame of the door.

I want to burst out what I'm holding in.

There is something.

All I ever want is you.

Alas, I save my words for when he gets back.

21

KEATS

Chewing on my pen, I skim the lines of the contract on my screen. Jotting down a quick note on my pad of paper, I'm grateful that I'm one paragraph away from being done. Sitting on a plane in first class for the morning red eye, I'm not loving the grueling week, even if I love working with the Spinners' general manager Vaughn Madden or the fact that Oliver is also present on this trip.

The thing about being the legal counsel for a hockey team is that there are always constant curves in the way you approach others in your work. It's not always straight and narrow. Contracts in relations to players are high stakes, and contracts with team sponsors require a bit more finesse.

Imagine that. I manage to transform my style in law, but when it comes to Esme, I lose my ability to adapt to situations. Such as being direct about what I'm *really* feeling.

That's probably with good reason since I know I want her, and we're not following any traditional timelines, but eventually that has to catch up to address the bigger picture.

Sighing and sinking back into my seat, I'm relieved that a week of schmoozing with sponsors is over. I even managed to cut a day out of this trip. Esme has been out like a light with the flu, and she kept repeating that my work life has impeccable timing because she isn't sure she could save me from the plague she has. Truthfully, I can't recall a day that I had to take off because I was sick. Not ever, actually.

And remembering the days when I wouldn't bother trying to get home at a reasonable hour seem long ago.

Actually, thinking outside of my work world is a new concept.

It's because of her.

She makes me laugh and keeps me in line.

A wildflower that sways in the wind and blows away the only focus in life I had and carries in the realization that I can have something outside of work that I apparently never imagined.

But now I do.

There is more to life, and it's spending it with someone.

A woman who makes me laugh, calls me out when needed, and surprises me at random moments.

It's turning me into an absolutely sappy guy who needs to bring a little edge back.

The corners of my mouth tug when I picture Esme passed out in bed with probably a little snore. Surprising her will hopefully make her happy. But then her words before I left still poke at me. She kind of insinuated that she will move back when her house is ready.

It makes sense. Complete sense.

She has a house. That's not something you can forget about.

Even if in a perverse way, I don't want her to have that house at all.

Having forgotten that Oliver is next to me, I startle when

he nudges my arm holding up his empty cup to the flight attendant to indicate for another water.

"You're smiling to yourself," he notes.

No point in hiding it. "Just thinking about how there is someone at home when I get there."

"That's good. Otherwise, it would be awkward."

Closing my laptop screen, I allow my thoughts to float in and out of my head. "Nah, we're good. Or rather we both appear content. I'm still trying to comprehend the best way to discuss what I might envision for the road ahead, but still…" A deep breath fills my lungs. "It's like my enjoyment is scraping along reality and they are both trying to win a fight."

Oliver stares at me blankly. "That's a positive?"

I shrug my shoulder, with my smile still glued to my face. "I haven't figured that out, either. Right now, I'm just going to head home." Glancing at my watch, I check the time. "I should make it back around nine."

"The benefit of living on the same street is that we can share the ride back. If you are nice then I'll let the driver drop you off first." He's messing with me, and since it's not even seven, I don't bother with a rebuff. "But seriously, I'm going to drop my stuff off then hit Foxy Rox for a decent coffee and breakfast then the gym. There is a hot new yoga instructor, and if I plan my timing right then I'll run into her."

"Bachelor life. Enjoy it." It doesn't appeal to me anymore.

He thanks the attendant for another water, and I shake my head to her to assure that I don't need anything.

Except Esme.

Oliver sips his drink. "Did the contractor start on her house?" he asks innocently, trying to make small talk. We were so busy during the last week that any downtime we had was reserved for sleep.

Scratching my cheek, I don't seem to enjoy the answer. "Yeah, but there are so many hiccups. Esme hasn't really checked up since she's been in bed sick." Maybe I should pick up medicine supplies on my way back.

"I'm curious what it will all look like in the end. Maybe these two houses getting a remodel will increase the property value on Everhope Road."

I turn my head to him with my face screwed. "You have some audacity. That's what you think of?"

His eyes widen. "Come on, I don't have an emotional connection like you, and I'm a business guy. It's a reasonable point to think about."

My head gently bounces side to side, as perhaps he has a point.

"Have you sent Mrs. Tiller thank-you flowers or a fruit basket or something? She created this forced living-together situation that you've got going on. You landed a girlfriend."

I scoff a laugh. "I would like to think that we were heading that way before the flames." Good old Mrs. Tiller just unbeknownst gave us a big shove in the right direction.

Direction.

That word again.

The clear-as-day answer seems to be hidden in a clue. Instead of a murder mystery party, it's plain, everyday life.

Esme has messed with my powers to keep it together under uncertain times. All cards are off the table when it comes to her. Unraveling her would probably be my biggest win yet.

We're both idiots

"What was that?"

Shit. Again, forgot Oliver is here, and apparently, I thought aloud.

"Nothing. Esme and I just have to hash out a few details." If we have to argue this then maybe that's our way.

But she needs to know that I don't want her to go anywhere.

I intend on laying it on the table so we will at least be on the same page.

WALKING INTO MY HOUSE, it's quiet. I'm grateful that Esme is a clean freak like me, so everything is in place except the coffee table which tends to have either a laptop or other papers. She taunts me for my little workspace, but she's guilty too for working there early in the morning.

I didn't text Esme since she's expecting me tomorrow, and the element of surprise is us.

I leave my bag and laptop at the bottom of the stairs, intending to grab them later. Her keys are in the bowl by the door and her car's out front, which means she's here.

Gently stepping up the stairs, I quietly make my way to the bedroom where the door is ajar. Peeking through, I can see that Esme is asleep. It causes me to half smile to myself. I don't worry about making noise as she seems to be a in a deep sleep. Taking a moment, I admire the view of Esme lying in bed on her stomach with her cheek smudging against the pillow and her hair in a messy bun. She's in one of my shirts, that's a bonus.

A few steps closer to the bed, my head cocks to the side as I study her. There is no way I'm waking her up. She's probably as exhausted as me. However, I can't help it. I silently lean down and glide the back of my hand gingerly along her cheek, careful not to wake this beautiful creature.

Maybe, I'll wake her after I shower. I need to shave, too.

Leaving Esme to rest, I walk to the master bathroom. I land right in front of the mirror. I look like hell, clearly exhausted, with short stubble to match. Grabbing my toothbrush from the holder next to the sink, I continue to look ahead.

As if it is a photo on the wall, my eyes pick up the speck of something in the corner, and my eyes drift down next to the sink.

Placing the toothbrush back into the holder, I stare dazed at the box.

In what feels like slow motion, I pick it up to bring the box in better view. Yep, I'm reading that right. My pulse begins to soar, and my chest feels as though it might burst. Swallowing, I notice the box is a little light.

Immediately, I begin to search, and it takes only two seconds.

Holy fuck.

Dropping the box, I grab the stick, and my eyes squeeze as they remain fixed on the test to have a better view.

I take a long moment standing frozen, while inside, I'm suddenly swarmed with emotions in a new way. Or I might be having a heart attack.

Which is why I drop the pregnancy test, not taking notice where it lands.

Instead, I rush out of the bathroom, only to pause and take one glance of Esme still asleep and oblivious to the fact that I'm here.

Maybe I'm being a coward, but my body is acting in shock and adrenaline.

Which is why I walk away and leave.

22
KEATS

Staring aimlessly at the stuffed monkey in my nephew's chubby little hand, I'm not sure if this is the right idea to collect my thoughts.

Summer shifts Bo on her lap as she sits next to me on the sofa at Foxy Rox, getting settled after just arriving.

"Why the sudden need to see Bo? I mean, don't get me wrong, I'm happy to pencil you in on his busy social calendar, but you just sounded insistent on the phone," my sister prods.

My eyes drop to my coffee mug in my hand, as I've been waiting a few minutes. "You said when I called that you were in the car not far from here," I explain, as though I'm not that crazy.

"Meh, true. I needed to hit the superstore off the highway for our monthly diaper stock-up." She makes funny faces at her son and coos to him. "Uncle Keats seems a little moody, no?"

Rolling my eyes, I get to the point and reach for my nephew. "Gimme."

Now my sister just seems perplexed as she hands over the

goods. "Uh, why am I handing over Bo? It's always a win to give my arms a rest, but you're acting *really* strange." Does it matter? She seems relieved to be able to reach for her drink on the coffee table without a struggle.

My nephew is drooling on my forearm, but it doesn't matter. He's supposed to bring me clarity. Help me break down these feelings swirling inside me and through my bones.

"It's just been a long week, and maybe I'm struggling to burn off the exhaustion. Thought it would be good to see a familiar face or two."

My sister studies me. "Okay, what happened?"

I roll my lips into my mouth to avoid telling her my predicament. "Nothing," I lie.

"Work?"

"Fine."

"Esme?"

"Under the weather with a cold."

My sister rests her elbow against the back of the couch as she patiently waits for me to say more. "Give Bo some of your oat cookie that you haven't touched." She motions with her head to the small plate next to my coffee.

I nod and pull off a piece, deciding against informing her that it's an energy protein cookie that they make in-house here. Bo will be flying later.

He squeals, and I look down to see crumbs already over my clothes. Holding him closer, I try to channel my inner turmoil, and my internal voice is not informing me what I want to hear, but I push it to the side.

However, it highlights that my plan is failing.

My arms shoot out to hand him back and his feet dangle as my sister collects him to return to her lap. "Okay, annoyed with my kid? Not cool."

Rubbing my face, I want to scream away the aggravation.

"Sorry. I'm just trying to figure something out and my nephew wasn't solving it."

Her eyes drop to my nephew then lift to me. "Well, he isn't even two. Apologies if his skillset isn't up to par."

Blowing out a breath, I'm being such an ass, and my little sister, the angel she is, just takes it in stride with a fond smile. "I might have hit a little roadblock," I admit.

Especially since the kid did chip away at clarity in my head. I was supposed to be scared away by the thought of having a child. It's me. My own kids have not been on the radar. Which is why this whole day is turning into one big roll down a hill where I will eventually crash.

It's an epiphany.

A future that I do want.

And I'm disappointed.

Finding the pregnancy test, which Esme clearly didn't tell me she even needed to take. I would say that makes me livid, except…

I'm purely upset because the test is negative.

That's the crazy part.

Not once have we discussed kids in relation to us. Yet here I am, disheartened because she's not pregnant. With my child. Because in the future it has to be her. There is nobody else that I envision the future with.

That test is the kick in the gut that I've been waiting for to enlighten what is past our current relationship status.

"Your roadblock?" My sister reminds me that she is waiting for an answer.

A domino is getting knocked over in my head. "I guess it isn't one at all," I realize aloud.

"Everything is good between you and Esme, right? I

mean, I like her, but I'm always team Keats first, you're my brother."

I lean in to touch her arm with appreciation. "I promise, we're fine." Maybe Esme views it differently, but right now, there is only one outcome I will allow.

"I would say living together unexpectedly can be a challenge, but it can also bring great things." She smiles, and she has experience since her fiancé was forced to move in due to a request in a will.

"But you and Nash already had history," I highlight.

She shakes her head confidently. "Doesn't matter. It can all still come together, even if you don't have a past."

"Always so wise," I say dryly before taking a sip of my now-cold coffee.

"You might even be a step ahead, as a new relationship is an open book, and you can start on page one together."

Okay, now this is getting too sappy. "Conversation done."

Summer laughs. "Ah, I love it. Being able to tease my brother about his romantic life is golden."

"Happy to provide entertainment."

She begins to gather their things. "On that note, I'm not sure if our quick visit helped in any way, but we need to go. I still need to hit the store and then get this one home before his afternoon nap."

I help search for the stuffed monkey and stand with her when it seems she is ready to leave. "Thanks for stopping by."

"Sure. Let me know when you are offering your babysitter duties. Or if you would like to go change Bo's diaper now, then by all means."

"You're good. I'm not really a fan of kids unless it's my nephew or my own."

My sister immediately pauses, and her eyes bug out. "Say what?"

I drag a hand across my face. "Nothing. We'll be in touch, I see Oliver over there." I divert us, and when I hug Summer, she still seems to be pondering if she heard my blunder correctly. Luckily, my nephew saves my ass and begins to fuss, indicating they need to leave.

As they leave and Summer quickly waves to Oliver, I turn to my friend.

"You're not at home?" Oliver asks as he wanders my way. I forgot he mentioned that he would be here later.

My brows rise as I struggle to return to a normal conversation. "Uh, yeah."

"No offense, but you look a little the worse for wear, and it's only been a few hours since I saw you. Did something happen?" Even with enlightenment now present in my life, he can't be far off that I could use a refresh with a shower and sleep.

I rub the back of my neck. "Nothing to worry about. I just thought I would let Esme sleep in peace, as she still seems to be recovering from her flu." And apparently is not pregnant, to my dismay.

"Makes sense. Liam will be here in a few minutes, are you going to stick around?"

"Maybe. But I probably need to get back since I just spent time with my sister."

While he quickly goes to the counter to place his order, I'm left to stew in my thoughts again.

I've been falling for Esme, but I could be a little more flawless in my execution of the sentiment.

I fucking love her. Absolutely love her.

It's obvious that she's everything that apparently I

wanted. The person I'll grow old with and argue with, only to have make-up sex every single time.

And not living with me? No way am I letting her move back to her house. I'll burn it down again if I need to.

This is why I've been so incredibly possessive and drawn to her. She's more than mine; she's everything.

I'll shake her until she admits that she is with me on this. I might have been the one to fall first for her, but I'm convinced she has been trailing right behind me and hopefully is caught up.

"Why are you smiling to yourself?" Oliver breaks into my thoughts.

My arms flop up then fall. "Damn it, can you please stop interrupting me when I'm thinking?"

"Crabby." He slides onto the lounge chair next to me. "But seriously, are you okay?"

The stretched line on my mouth returns. "More than."

He takes a sip of coffee and seems to be skeptical but follows along. "I would ask if your current radiant state has to do with Esme, but I know that answer."

Staring ahead, I can't hold it any longer. "I'm going all in." I blink from my daze, and my eyes swim to Oliver who just shrugs as if it's nothing.

"For someone who spent years in law school, I've been wondering why you haven't already planned everything out once the lust clears." He cooly drinks his coffee as though this is a daily conversation.

"One day you will understand. You just have to wait for the right one, and then it will suddenly make sense."

Now Oliver's face puzzles. "Did they put something in your coffee here?" He pretends to search the room. "You are a little too positive for even me."

There is no other way to be. I'm tired of going in circles,

and Esme is at home probably having had a hellish few days if it led her to take a test.

Rubbing my face, I'm thankful that a giant dose of oxytocin will keep me going today.

"Just let me be. I'm going to head out. I really need to keep the day moving before I pass out." And I don't plan on wasting any more seconds.

Esme is at home, and unlucky for her, this is all going to go one way.

My way.

23
ESME

Pulling the pie out of the oven, I'm proud of myself. The kitchen smells of baked cherries, and first glance at my creation, I can see that the crust is just right with a golden sheen. Later, I'll add on some ice cream, and this will be complete.

Waking up at eleven in the morning, I felt refreshed, or rather I refuse to spend another day in bed at the mercy of a virus that's been taking me down for the count. I'm on the mend enough, and baking a pie feels fitting considering where my mind has been.

I saw Keats's bags at the bottom of the stairs, and to be honest, the overbearing sense that he was near seeped through my body when I woke. It's the faint aroma of his cologne and the air feeling less chilly. He must have had to run to the office and didn't want to wake me. Or even headed to the gym which is why I haven't bothered texting. He's back a day early, and me being knocked out in bed probably already ruined his surprise.

Setting the dish on the wire rack, I shuffle my hands out of the oven mitts and graze my finger on the top of the pie to check the crust. Or rather boost my confidence of my talented hobby.

Underneath keeping myself busy lies the true meaning for baking. I want to do something for Keats. The time away from one another has been enlightening for me. My thoughts began to line up, and the way I missed him even for a few days has only proven that I would miss him in the future, too.

A pie is a perfect symbol of our new beginning. He is more than worthy of one of my pies.

The sound of the door opening down the hall causes my subtle smile to beam. Grabbing the nearby kitchen towel, I squish it around the pie dish to lift up and display my gift. Turning around as Keats enters, my smile turns to a frown.

He slowly saunters to the kitchen island, keeping the counter as a barrier between us. Fear runs through me, tightening my heart. Keats appears serious, and it concerns me. There are no open arms or welcoming cunning grins. Instead, he stares at me with his chin gruff and his eyes heavy, slicing through me.

"I can't fight the reality anymore," he states.

Swallowing, nerves take over.

Plop.

The pie drops to my feet.

"Shit." My eyes sink down to the splattered red and gold. That's going to be hell to clean up, but I'll worry about that later. "Uh, I made you a pie." I smile nervously in an attempt to break the tense air.

Finally, he steps closer, and his face relaxes. "I can see that." He smirks.

I roll a shoulder back, swimming my eyes in all directions except straight at him. "It turns out that I like you a lot, which means you finally get a pie," I attempt to joke.

"I finally deserve one?"

Nodding my head, I remind myself that I woke up intent of being the spitfire that I've always been around him. "I can't hide it anymore."

My mind turns flustered at all of the disappointment inside me because he seems different, as though his reality isn't my own.

Keats steps closer. "Me neither, and when I saw the pregnancy test..."

I gulp air. *Shit. Shit. Shit.*

How could I forget about that?

"It's not what you think. It's negative, and I was just trying to figure out if I've been good old-fashioned sick or if the stress of the house caused me to forget one or two pills." I hold my hands up as if I need to defend myself. "But it's negative," I assure him.

"I'm kind of pissed about that."

My eyes bug out. Okay, forget every warm and fuzzy feeling that I had when I woke up. That spell has now been broken, and I clench my fists at my sides. "Are you kidding me? Last I checked it's a mutual risk when you decide to put your cock inside me," I sneer.

Keats's mouth slants to the side as he scratches his neck, not at all concerned that he has unleashed my inner disdain that once swirled inside me before I fell hard for this guy. "This is unbelievable, to think that I made you a pie." I shake my head in astonishment for the turn of events. My finger darts out and points at him. "You don't deserve a pie."

Keats charges forward, flips my wrists and holds them up, with his eyes now cutting right through me.

"Woman, calm down," he grits out. He blows out an aggravated breath. "Of course, this would turn into an argument. It's you." My entire mouth gapes open, even though his tone isn't harsh, it's the opposite. I try and struggle out of his, admittedly, seductive move. "I'm pissed because it's negative."

What?

I still, and my eyes flutter, trying to ensure that I heard him right or if licking the bowl of dough earlier is causing me to think unrealistically. "W-what?" I stammer out.

His hands remain wrapped around my wrists. He should be laughing now because he's joking. Why isn't he doing that? "For some reason… I was disappointed that it's negative."

My nose lifts up because I'm still in disbelief. "Why?" He steps between my legs and walks me back to trap me between his body and the counter. The pressure of his palms is a little less, but he won't let me go.

"Because apparently you're the one I want to spend my future with," he rasps as his eyes dip down to my mouth and his thumb circles my cheek with a sly look, causing goosebumps to rise on my body. "It's clear as day now. I'm so completely in love with you. You're everything I want in the future that I never realized how much I crave. In simple terms, Esme, I love you. I fucking love you."

The balloon of irritation from the last few minutes pops, and my entire body sags in relief. Elation spreads through me, and my smile creeps up. "I love you too. I thought our domestic bliss was confusing me, or because we're stuck in the same place, sometimes a routine. Maybe unable to think past the now. I was waiting for hints that it wasn't a one-sided thing."

"This is a big fucking hint, no?"

My mouth might hurt from how wide my lips are stretching in a long line up. "I would say so."

Keats captures my lips and kisses me fiercely, like the many times that he has claimed me all for himself. This time is different, it's a permanent stamp that this is us for the long haul. I surrender my breath and lips to him as I scream with joy inside.

The slow parting of lips is only bearable because now we can speak freely.

"So yeah, I'm not angry about the test, only disappointed it's negative, even though we are nowhere near ready to be parents, and now I'm pissed because there is a pie on the floor after months of waiting." He grins.

I pinch his stomach at the way my man who used to be stern, grumpy, and insufferable is now lighthearted around me. "I know, it's gooey and between my toes."

Our eyes fall to see that somewhere during our stormy minute that I unknowingly stepped into dessert.

Keats laughs, and his answer to my predicament is to hoist me up until my behind is sitting on the counter.

"Sounds like us." He combs strands of my hair behind my ear, and his eyes with a lust-filled gleam lock with mine. "Maybe before I left earlier in the week, I wasn't thrilled at the reminder that you actually live next door."

"Kind of. We seem to have mailboxes next to one another. And if you're lucky, I might purposely not-so-accidentally send things to your address, which means you might have to deal with me more. Hope you don't mind." I nibble my bottom lip.

His tongue darts to the corner of his mouth. "Next door feels too far away, but I know you own the house." He doesn't sound enthused.

"Doesn't mean it's a home." The tips of my fingers come up to touch his jaw and keep his view on me. "It's not going to be a fast fixer-upper, and for all I know, they will tell me that I need to replace something else. Lucky for me, I have an amazing host who will let me stay, and I want to stay... for a really long time." I place a tender kiss on his lips.

"Damn straight."

Another kiss and another.

"Remember when we went to the field near the stream?" He nods at my words. "We talked about life just moving but missing a piece. Now, it's very clear that I was missing you. You make it exciting, and my life feels better."

He stares affectionately at me with his fingers tucking another strand of hair behind my ear. "Wildflowers. I thought of that moment too on the airplane. No longer my little demon, you're the one I needed all along to be a somewhat decent man." He smiles softly to himself.

"You are a little more than decent. I'm lucky, and you take care of me. I'm spirited and keep you on your toes. We both bring something to the table... which absolutely should not have any work papers on it."

He drops his head forward so our foreheads bump together. "Esme."

"I like the way you say my name. I don't think I've ever heard someone say it that way. You shouldn't be so tender. It never crossed my mind that someone can say it in a way that makes me theirs, and that's what I want."

"You *are* mine."

Then it escalates, and Keats begins to tug on my yoga pants, and my fingers fiddle with his jeans.

He ruthlessly drags off everything from my waist down, and he lowers his pants just enough. I'm lost in this moment and wrap my legs around his waist, and he drives right into me, causing me to yelp.

"I love you," he breathes into my ear.

"I love you," I rasp back before a moan escapes my lips.

My arm circles around his neck to give me stability, and

he keeps my hips square and aligned to his as he plunges in and out of me. Our mouths suck when they meet and our teeth bite when we follow the map of one another's necks.

I could break into pieces purely because of how hard we are confirming the shift of our relationship. Also, because an orgasm is about to hit me like a tidal wave.

Neither of us are quiet, and our bodies knock on the counter with every thrust. Dizziness swirls in my head as my body is light but my heart a weight as this man is a rock that is unable to be moved, and that's the only way I want it.

"I think I might black out," Keats pants out.

I don't get a chance to answer as my orgasm rips through me which brings on his own. We both end up unable to move, and I'm confident that I can hear the racing of his heart. My head falls to his shoulder as I remain straddled around him. Keats grips the edge of the counter like he might collapse.

Our heavy breathing can't seem to shallow out, which just means we remain like this longer. My fingers draw on his back, and his jaw rests on my cheek.

"I might not survive keeping you forever," he jokes.

"Old man," I answer lazily.

Keats chuckles gruffly. "I like this smell. Sweat mixed with a pie-fumed kitchen."

"Weird but fine." My lips pout out then fall. "Oh no! Your pie."

"It's okay, you have plenty of time in the future to make me a new one."

"If you behave," I tease.

We stay in this embrace until gravity hits, and Keats pulls up his jeans and swoops up my panties from the floor. I put them on then grab the nearby kitchen towel to wipe my feet. "We should jump in the shower, and I'll clean this up later." I glance down to the travesty on the floor.

"Come on." He turns his back to me and invites me to jump on for a piggyback. As cute as it is, it's practical too since my feet are still sticky.

In the shower, we stand together under the water, with steam filling the room and hands on one another's backs. We haven't bothered yet with lathering soap.

"Are you feeling better?" he asks, and he must mean from my virus.

"You didn't get the memo that I was in the kitchen baking up a storm? But yeah, I'm feeling better. I'll probably need to head to bed early, though."

Keats releases a calm sigh. "We're all good on the clarification front? Need me to lay out any more terms?"

I stifle a laugh. "You just walked into a lawyer joke there that I shall not say. And no, all bright as day."

He slaps my ass, and I squeal from surprise. "Good. I like when you listen the first time."

I peer up to him. "Can you still say it again?"

"I love you." His tone is delicate.

I wrap my arms tighter around him and nuzzle into his chest for a few beats. "We've been on an adventure, you and I. I'm not sure I've really thought about my future with anyone until you came along. It doesn't scare me, but I was still afraid to say the words. As much as I'm defiant and stand my ground, I was waiting for you to lead the way."

Keats kisses my forehead. "Don't do that again. The games are over."

"Our truce," I lament.

Pulling me flush, I get the clue to climb up and bind my legs around his middle. He takes a few steps, and I feel the coolness of the tile against my back. "Trust me, when your house is ready, you won't move. It will be too far away from me, and you'll hate it."

The tightening of my cheeks brings about my knowing grin. "Bossy yet probably true. We shall see."

He ogles his eyes at me. "Don't challenge me."

Keats doesn't need to. Still, I should probably bring reason. "We've established what we are and that we will take it one step at a time." Keeping a straight face, internally I believe I'm already three steps ahead. He kisses me again, and I feel his cock between us. "Really? Another round?"

He's amused as he places me back on my feet and guides me to ensure I'm fully under the water again. "Nah, I'll let you rest."

"Phew, I enjoy just lying in bed with you and staring at each other," I say as I grab the shampoo bottle.

Keats grows quiet, and I glance over my shoulder as he watches me with fondness. "I kind of like the way we got here. To this point, I mean. You think we'll build from this?"

Be still my heart. This man is head over heels in love with me.

"It will only get better," I promise.

24

KEATS

Esme seems content as we sit inside Foxy Rox for a bite to eat. It's the weekend and Esme just got back from Chicago where she spent the night there for a girls' evening. Last night, I missed our routine of me on my laptop for an hour or two of work while Esme goes a little crazy on the cleaning and house organization front, something I've learned during the last six weeks that she loves to do. We both end up in bed defeated and watch a movie before we have sex every day.

Now, I'm watching her smile as she watches people through the window walk by on Main Street. "Hailey is lucky. The bridesmaid dress for Liam's wedding that she had to try on last night is elegant. She's been spared horrendous dresses." My lips press together, and I only nod. "Anyway, Hailey mentioned that she heard on the Everhope grapevine that there might be a new restaurant opening down on the river. Family-style eating with specialty corn bread. I guess that appeases the older crowd and the young families popping up in Everhope."

I've only heard half her words because I'm anticipating

this afternoon. The conversation that's been a long time coming.

She does a double take when she must notice that I'm caught in a daze. "What's up with you? You've been quiet, and they have Babka on the menu today. Even you can't pass up the twist of chocolate dough."

The corner of my mouth tugs. "Sorry, just lost in thought."

Her lips wrap around the straw of her drink, and to my surprise, she doesn't dig for answers. "It's great that the builders are putting in a little extra time on the weekends to move along my house. I should really start to order furniture."

I don't need that reminder. "Right." My T is sharp.

It causes her to chortle a laugh. "Just focus on your onion bagel with egg salad. I'm very familiar with what's brewing in your head."

"What might that be?" I ask before I take a bite of my lunch.

"The living situation. I mean, I know it will be odd going back and forth or deciding whose bedroom to sleep in every night, but… it is what it is." Such a liar she is.

We've only briefly discussed the several options of what to do. Sell, rent, live separately. I'm positive of what she wants, but to my surprise, she seems shy to admit her wish.

I'll just decide for her. Informing her of our fate will not be discussed in the town coffee joint where the new kindergarten teacher is getting hit on by the firefighter and a two-year-old just threw a muffin.

Our serious relationship move calls for my ability to impress and us alone in private.

"Esme, relax. Just enjoy your blueberry bagel with strawberry cream cheese and don't tell me that it meets your daily fruit intake." I give her a knowing look while her mouth is stuffed with food.

"Fair enough. I forgot that my boyfriend only deals with serious matters behind closed doors, or rather places that make it easy for him to fuck me into agreement." It sounds muffled as she's still chewing, but I understand enough.

I grin as I scan the place and venture a glance through the window for the view. A few months ago, I would have said that grabbing lunch at the quaint coffee spot, with a stop at the grocery store on the way home while discussing if we should throw in a load of laundry, was my idea of hell.

Not anymore.

Esme makes it fun, and I don't use that word lightly.

"We received the details for the hotel room for Liam's wedding. I'll book the tickets to Colorado once your assistant confirms with you what time you can get away for the flight. It will be off-season for the Spinners; do you think we can add an extra day or two to the trip?"

Point proven. We are in joint calendar planning. A serious relationship step.

"I don't see why not." I shrug.

She smiles brightly. "Perfect. It will be a change of scenery and a little romantic getaway."

My wry smile doesn't fade as my attention remains on the afternoon ahead.

Pretending to check the time on my watch, I tell her, "We should get going if you want to chat with the builders before they leave."

Esme finishes with her napkin and nods. "You are totally right."

I pay the check, and we walk down Main Street with the clouds now out. It always makes me laugh that they still have the old parking meters. Who the hell carries around quarters these days?

Our drive back is simple and quiet. I bet that Esme is beat after last night, and well, I'm silent because I'm replaying the plan in my head.

As we drive down Everhope Road, I can see in the distance that the crew are busy packing up their truck. "Just in time," I note.

Pulling up, I press the button to lower Esme's window. We could park and get out of the car, but this just seems easier.

"Hey, Esme," Steven says.

"Thanks for working what feels like around the clock. I'll have a look later. Anything major that I should know about?"

The guy winces and does his best to avoid Esme's face as he rubs the back of his neck. "Well, we're going to have to rewire again, as it seems a squirrel or raccoon bit through the wire. Maybe a rat even."

"What!" She shrieks, horrified, and even I find the thought pretty disgusting. "We have rats on this street?"

Stretching my upper body, I lean closer to speak. "Surely, you're joking, right?"

"Could be. Either way, some animal is determined to set us back." He throws his thumb over his shoulder. "Then we have the crew that the Tiller family hired. We have to coordinate when they are filling in cement or need to use machinery that might affect space. We're treading along but slowly."

Esme grumbles a sound and slouches her shoulders as she sits back and clicks open her seatbelt. "This is not what I wanted to hear."

It's completely what I wanted to hear.

Adds more fuel to the fire that I'm lighting today.

"Well, we'll be back tomorrow. We're going to start a little later since my guys worked extra today."

Esme nods in understanding, and I lift my hand from the wheel to wave. "Thanks. I know you are doing your best."

At a snail's pace, I drive up a few feet to the mailboxes. "Can you check that? I'm expecting some documents."

She rolls her eyes to glance sidelong at me. "Really? I just received *that* news and now you want to harass me about our old game that terrorized the neighborhood?"

I manage to keep my laugh under my breath, and Esme doesn't seem to enjoy my humor due to the last ten minutes.

But it all changes when we park and walk inside. Instantly, I step behind her, with my hands covering her eyes. "Close your eyes," I tell her.

She snickers. "Uh, you are kind of doing that for me. What's going on?"

Smiling to myself, I walk her forward down the hall toward the laundry room. I stop us right at the doorway to the small office that I never use.

My hands fall from her face and already I'm proud of my efforts.

Esme takes a few moments to flicker her eyes and adjust to her surroundings before she halfway turns to face me with confusion on her face. "What is this?"

Swooping up her wrists, I drag her along further into the room, her smile inching wider. "Your mood desk."

She's assessing the scene, and I'm along for the ride and following her view. A new desk with space for her computer, candles, a string of those white party lights, a cactus, and a few photos of her blown up and placed in frames that are hanging on the wall. Her entire face is in awe and still trying to comprehend what I've done.

"This is so sweet." Her fingertips touch my arm, and my

heart warms because I wanted to do this gesture for her, and I'm pleased she seems happy. But then she swats my arm. "Leave it to you to pick those photos for the wall."

I yank her close so her back is to my front as I embrace her with my arms around her belly. "That was your mistake for sending me those sexy photos of you in nothing but a sheet a while ago."

She laughs, and it sounds so jubilant. "You realize that you can never let anyone enter this room."

"It also kind of means that you have a place that's a little more permanent here," I whisper into her ear. Esme quiets, but her body doesn't tense. "I'm not sure why I didn't think of this sooner, to be honest."

"Because I was supposed to be here temporarily even if we are madly in love. No pressure." Her tone is floaty.

"Not anymore. You're moving in. As in staying here and not leaving. I'll get the bed ties if I need to."

"I didn't hear a question in what you just said." She turns in my arms, her face poised and my look cunning.

My hand shoots up to cup her cheek and print my thumb onto her pillowy bottom lip. "I don't need to. I've made the decision for you."

Esme begins to smirk. "We should really assess your demanding and in-control-of-our-relationship aspect. But lucky for you, it's what I want. This is all why I magnetize to you."

"You're my good girl." There is an underlying lightheartedness. "You've been thinking about this decision, and as much as we might say that there are several scenarios that could happen, you've only ever wanted one of those, and me too. So, you're moving in on a permanent basis."

She purrs a breath and slides her arms up to latch onto my neck with her eyes tipped up while I look down to meet her.

"Since I don't get to answer, then it seems as though this is happening… I was going to demand it too. You just beat me to it."

"Damn straight." I dive down to steal a kiss, and I can't help myself and let my hands wander lower to squeeze her ass. "Practical me needs to inform you that you're still going to have to do something with that house."

"I'll probably rent it out. I haven't decided yet. Hailey mentioned that she's looking for a place. We don't need to think about that now. We have animals intent on ruining the house, probably possessed by that evil spirit that once lived there, and I have a boyfriend to do wicked things with me on a hard surface." I'm never going to be disappointed by the way as Esme is insatiable and can keep up with my own level of needs.

"Not the desk." I'm serious. "It took me an hour last night to figure out where the hell to place candles and Post-its and all of that stuff."

She chuckles. "Your wish is my command."

Our next kiss is longer with more intention. We're becoming something longer lasting, she and I.

Her lips drag along mine. "I love you," she reminds me, and her voice is husky and sexy, and God, I'm going to lay her down on our bed to make love to her slowly.

"You may have a house next door but it's no longer a home. Your home is here."

Our teeth scrape against one another as our noses nuzzle. "It's the truth, and I'm well aware. I was going to share this all when I brought you your coffee and we somehow got in a lovers' quarrel where I burst out what I'm feeling."

My head falls back as I laugh because not one word of that is sarcasm. It's 100% Esme. "We can still role play that if you want."

She puckers her lips to the side as she pretends to consider. "Nah, lying in bed and telling you how sweet this all is sounds better."

I kiss the top of her head. "I'll tell you that I love you over and over."

"Our usual weekend then."

"Now you're officially living here and never leaving."

Her smirk turns mischievous. "Why are we still talking about this?" She steps back and offers me her hand. "Come on, as much as I'm going to enjoy your fine work, we need a bed right now."

Lunging forward, I pick her up and throw her over my shoulder fireman style. "Say no more. I've exceeded surprise expectations and can now be rewarded."

Esme kicks her feet. "Fuck off, Keats. You can reward me for agreeing to stay." She's so unbelievably giddy and giggly right now.

Swinging her around before ascending the stairs, I pretend to be aggravated. "Don't even start. I'm going to tape your mouth shut."

"Ooh, wrists too? Please say my wrists." She's half teasing but also wants it.

I love this woman, and our future looks very promising.

EPILOGUE: KEATS

8 MONTHS LATER

Tossing my suit jacket onto the corner chair in the hotel room, I'm relieved we can hit the mattress. Turning my head, I see Esme throwing her shoes carelessly onto the floor. She lost the heels already two hours ago while dancing at Liam's wedding.

"I'm not sure who was drunker, Liam's uncle or Ava's cousin." She has a bewildered face.

"The Irish always win, so Liam's uncle for sure." I unbutton my shirt, my entire body feeling heavy. "At least we kept it together."

She walks to me and presents her back as my cue to unzip her dress. Knee-length and turquoise were a solid choice, and the lack of bra even better.

Esme snickers. "Alcohol-wise, but our feet will be killing us tomorrow."

I place a soft kiss on her shoulder as her dress pools at her feet. "Luckily, brunch for out-of-town guests isn't until 10:30, so we can sleep in."

We explored Sage Creek yesterday when we arrived in Colorado and grabbed a coffee at Smokey Java's over on Main Street this morning. So we'll feel no guilt on our part if we skip tourist activities tomorrow morning.

I unbuckle my pants as Esme circles toward me, and I'm rewarded with the view of her near naked body, with her breasts pert and nipples peaked, and her sly smile is hot as hell. Stepping closer, I encase my arms around her with a sound rumbling in my throat.

"Am I your prize since you didn't catch the bouquet?" Doesn't matter. I'll ask her to marry me anyway very soon.

She lifts her finger and plants it on my lips to shush me. "It seems I've gotten something better."

One step closer and I break away from her finger. I kiss her lips long and smooth while I walk us to the foot of the mattress. As soon as the back of Esme's knees hit the bed, I lie her down, hovering over her and settling between her open thighs.

"We're going to be so tired tomorrow," I whisper, though I'm not deterred as I tug on her panties.

"Worth it," she rasps and bucks her hips up to help me remove the last scrap of fabric on her body.

I nuzzle into her neck, smelling the faint remainder of her perfume, and my teeth graze her skin. "I love you," I murmur into her body.

"Imagine that, I love you, too."

We made it quick that round before we both fell victim to our sleepy slumber, tangled around one another. But waking up is a different story.

Slow kisses and hands roaming for minutes, our eyes locked, and we said nothing with the sun brightening the room, as we forgot to close the second curtain. Esme has a beautiful glow. Especially when we end up in the middle of the bed, both sitting up and her body on top of my lap as I piston up inside her.

I hold her hips firm, and her hands rest on my shoulders. Our heavy breathing fills the room, and a scolding warmth radiates from our skin. I guide her to continue to bounce on top of me, her breasts pressed against my bare chest. The white sheet that was wrapped around us is now a knotted mess somewhere near my feet.

"Esme, I'm almost there," I say against her lips.

Her breath trails from my mouth down along my cheekbone and then right to my ear. "Me too."

I can feel her tighten, and I move fast, more robust as I thrust into her. If the room next door doesn't hear us orgasm, then they should fucking check their hearing.

Esme and I move together until we both find a release that has been building since the moment she sat on my lap, taunting me with her tits and her hair thrown behind her shoulders. Such a beauty.

With my heart about to explode as I remain inside of her, attempting to return to a normal breath, I'm surprised I don't fall back. But I always like it when Esme falls apart then rests her cheek against my shoulder as we take a few moments to return to earth.

"Marry me," she asks, exhausted.

Guess I'm not returning to earth quite yet.

Blinking my eyes, I'm not sure I heard her right. "Say what?"

She doesn't move an inch. "Marry me."

Now I'm wide awake. I set my hands on her upper arms to

encourage her to create space. Our eyes meet, and Esme is completely unreadable.

"Marry me." Her tone has turned anxious.

I blankly stare at her. "You've mentioned."

She balks at me, eyes wide.

"No."

Her face falls. "W-what?"

"No. You have impeccable timing. Really? You can't ask me while my cock is still inside you."

"That makes it all the better," she says, and her voice squeaks.

I splay my hands against her back to keep her in place as a smirk begins to draw on my mouth. "And no, you can't ask me."

"Why not?" she protests.

"Because that's my role, and we are going to do it my way."

Her jaw drops. "I ask you to marry me and this is what you say?"

Esme slides off of me, and I follow her off the bed. Standing up, we face one another, completely naked. This isn't how Sunday was supposed to go. "I'm saying that I'm saying no to you."

She points her finger at me. "So you don't want to marry me?" She looks like she is about to burst into tears.

I don't step forward in a flash, choosing to stay in place to watch my beautiful Esme about to go from fearful to elated. "I do want to marry you. That's why I had planned to ask you when we got back. So yeah, you can't ask me to marry you. We are going traditional, and I'm the one to ask."

Her eyes flutter as she stares at me. "Really?" She seems to doubt me.

"Yeah, really." I grab a fresh pair of boxer briefs from the open suitcase as it sinks in for her.

"You're not just saying that? I mean, we are at a wedding, so maybe we are both wrapped up in the wedding fever."

"Is that why you asked?" Now, I'm a little concerned.

She shakes her head frantically. "No. It's just the words rolled out of my mouth. Maybe this weekend has been a little confronting… for what I want. Which is you, a future, you as my husband, babies one day."

I pause and take a breath. "Esme," I grit out because I'm kind of annoyed that she's taken away the element of surprise in our future.

My mouth tightens, and I bite my bottom lip, but I grabbed her attention and now she's trying to read my face.

"What?" she wonders

"I was going to ask you to marry me next week." Her eyes grow and her lips part, but no words come. "I even have the ring ready. My sister helped me pick it."

Her mouth goes slack. "W-what?"

I walk toward her slowly. "I had this whole thing planned. I was going to leave the ring in the mailbox for you to find. We would have a family BBQ to surprise you. I mean, we can still have the BBQ since I have a sandbox in my yard, and it needs my nephew to play in it… maybe one day our own kid too."

She stammers for a second but then rushes to me, cups my face, and slams her lips onto mine. "Yes." That was the most overzealous answer I've ever heard, and it causes my grin to appear.

"I didn't even ask."

She swats my shoulder. "Then why the hell tell me that tidbit of information? So, yes."

My eyes squinch at her. "I can't even actually ask?"

"No. I say yes."

I have to laugh now. Stubborn Esme is one of the best things to experience. Or at least when we are not disputing about the shopping list for the week.

"Well then, looks like I have gained myself a fiancée." I pull her close to bring our bodies flush, and her warm smile invites me in for another kiss. It's a sensual kiss until it's broken.

Her face sours. "Wait, you didn't just feed me that spiel about a ring to ease me, did you?"

Rolling my eyes, I hope we don't go in circles. "I'm marrying you, so deal with it."

She studies me for a few seconds. "Fine. We can get married," she theatrically agrees.

I pinch her sides which draws out a giggle, and I yank her close only to toss her back onto the bed. I join her by lying on my side to face her.

My fingers feather down her cheek. "A wife. Babies. We'll have it all."

"I'm your fiancée," she whispers.

"Yeah, you are."

She shimmies closer and nuzzles into my body. "Will you still ask me again? With the whole mailbox proposal. I'll pretend you never asked yet."

"But I have asked." Now, I'm just messing with her. I'll do it all for her. She pinches my side. "Ouch."

Esme kisses me. "This calls for congratulations sex. But we are on a schedule and have to get to brunch."

I smirk at her. "Brunch might have to wait." I flip her to her back. "I would like to remind you that you're everything I wanted."

Esme hooks her leg over my hip. "I might have a few minutes to spare."

SHE SHAKES me off as I kiss the base of her neck as we walk into the elevator. We have ridiculous giddy grins, and I can't stop touching her. She'll look even better when my ring is on her finger.

"We'll be only a few minutes late for brunch, so we're fine." She presses the button for the lobby.

But our eyes lift when the sound of someone rushing to join us causes me to hold the door from closing.

Oliver steps in and seems to be acting strangely. "Good morning, you two."

"Wait!" The sound of Hailey's voice prevents us from hitting the button to close.

She too joins us. Hailey gives an odd look to Oliver before she smiles at Esme and me.

The doors close, and the quiet is unnerving.

Oliver and Hailey are intent on looking forward. Esme watches them then throws me a puzzled look.

"Seems we all had eventful mornings," I comment and slyly smile.

Oliver shoots me a death stare.

"I hope there are waffles. I'm dying of hunger," Esme says while she no longer takes notice of the rest of us.

Hailey nervously rolls her lips in and seems to study the numbers lighting up above the door.

"I bet Oliver has worked up an appetite."

"Keats," Oliver growls.

Hailey zooms her gaze to Esme. "You told him?"

"You told her?" Oliver accuses me.

Esme raises her arms. "Told who what?"

We all look at one another, but most of all, Oliver and Hailey stare at each other before both of their shoulders fall.

"I told Keats," Oliver deflates.

Hailey shrugs. "I told Esme."

Esme begins to chuckle under her breath. "Ah, classic. You think Keats and I told one another that you two might have… well… built up an appetite due to your roadtrip adventures."

I laugh with Esme, but Oliver and Hailey don't find it humorous.

"Can we just not talk about this? It's Liam's wedding weekend, and I just want to focus on omelets." Hailey huffs.

"I kind of feel I need to have a bet going for how long it will be before Liam figures out that you two, well…"

"It was one night!" they shout in unison.

Esme winces. "*Yeah…* I'm not buying that." The elevator dings open, and I follow Esme out who stops to glance over her shoulder at Oliver and Hailey standing motionless in the middle of the elevator. "Hailey caught the bouquet last night. If you two are looking for a discussion topic." She grins cheekily.

We both walk away, leaving them behind.

I wrap my arm around Esme from the side and kiss her cheek. "We didn't tell them our news."

"Meh. You can wow them later in the week after your other proposal. How is that going to go again?"

"Geez, no element of surprise."

THANK YOU

To readers, thank you for taking a chance on Esme and Keats. Writing about small towns that remind me of where I grew up is always fun. It's also because of readers that my adventure as a writer continues. To my editor, Lindsay, who has been with me from book one; to my cover designer, Lindsey, for helping me imagine the story; to Autumn for beta reading; and to Rachel for the other set of eyes and all the conversations. Coffee, can I thank a drink? I should. Of course, my family allows me to use my chaotic schedule to write. Anyone, who played a part on this book, you hold a spot in my heart. To the next one!

Made in the USA
Monee, IL
04 August 2025